GIVE THEM A REASON TO HATE YOU SHAWTY

A Hood Love Story

TONYA WILLIAMS

SHAN Presents

Subscribe

Text Shan to 22828 to stay up to date with new releases, sneak peeks, contest, and more....

Submissions

To submit your manuscript to Shan Presents, please send
the first three chapters and synopsis to
submissions@shanpresents.com

Synopsis

23-year-old Courtney Adams is dating one of the highest paid plugs in the city. That is until she's introduced to his boss, the connect, Adric "AD" Hernandez. Her best friend Britin was the one to introduce them, for her own selfish motives. They say, you never know who's your real friend until you meet a man that gives you the world. Will Courtney and Britin's friendship overcome Britin's jealousy for the way that men loves Courtney?

Paiton "Slade" Perez is one of the most successful drug dealers to come out of the Perez Cartel Organization, but he must give credit for his success to his connect, Adric Hernandez. His day one, Jeremiah, is a wolf in sheep's clothing, wanting Courtney for himself, and going against Slade's wishes.

Adric "AD" Hernandez is every girl's problem solver. He's charismatic, fit, fine, and swimming in money. Yet, no woman in Atlanta can bag him, except for simple ass Courtney Adams. When word gets out that she's the one that he's chosen to be with, his ex and her nemesis starts plotting heavily on how to break things up between them.

He knows who and what he wants but will their love story be too hood to survive the secrets that stand in between them?

Take a read inside to find out the fate of these lovers and their friendships.

Courtney

"Come on Brit! Let's hurry up and go in this store before these niggas try and stop us. You know they be thirsty as fuck." I looked over to my right at my best friend, who was reapplying her foundation in my sun visor.

I rolled my eyes at this bitch cause I'd stopped at the convenient store in the hood, and there wasn't nothing but bum ass niggas posted 'round the corner of the store tryna get at us cause we were on some hot girl shit this summer. I smacked my lips and opened my driver door to leave her where the fuck she was at. All I wanted to do was be on some bald-headed hoe shit.

"Wait! Hold up girl! Don't leave me!" Britin yelled.

"Well, you better bring yo ass on then!" I screamed from behind me.

"Aye shawty! Who-dee-who!" This light skinned dude that was tatted up screamed from the passenger side of his homeboy's whip.

"Ugh uhn! I ain't got time!" I looked back and waved my hands at him.

I felt like the baddest bitch in the city at that moment, cause the niggas had me feeling like Trina. I started reciting the lyrics to her song, *Look Back at Me*, in my head as I twisted my fat ass inside of the convenient store. I'd stopped to gas up my 2010 gray Honda Accord, but a bitch had the munchies, and we were headed to the hood. One thing I hated doing was walking 'round to the hood store. I always posted up in one spot and stood there acting bad and boujee wit my bitch Britin. She'd entertain these other niggas, but I'd curve every single one of them. Only a boss could get me, but these niggas knew not to mother fuckin try me. I'm the girlfriend of one of the highest paid plugs in the city. Paiton "Slade" Perez is my nigga.

I was holding the door open for Britin when it felt like the ground beneath me started to shake. I jerked my head back and walked back out the door of the convenient store to see who it was bumpin their music loud like that. It was some hood niggas in expensive ass whips, parking and showing off their cars at the store. I pressed my lips together and just stared at them. About three different niggas lifted the doors of their rides and hopped out to sit on top of the hoods of their cars. They were flashy with their flashy ass whips, but I already had my nigga, so I wasn't stuntin none of them. But him... the mixed, tall,

Mexican or Puerto Rican one with the smile and muscular arms... he could get it. He winked his eye at me, so I hurried up and turned my ass around to walk inside of the store to get my snacks and pay for my gas. I had to get the hell out of there.

"Girl! Did you see the way that Puerto Rican dude was looking at you out there?" Britin loudmouth ass asked me as we were walking up the candy aisle.

"Um uhn! Ion know what you talkin bout," I told her as I grabbed a bag of rainbow Skittles and started up the aisle to walk to the checkout counter.

I stopped dead in my tracks before I could make it up the aisle to pay for my candy. It was him; he was standing in front of me. I felt like I was about to sink into the concrete of the floor. I couldn't find the words to say to him, but I couldn't let him know that I thought that he was fine as shit, so I said what I had to say to him.

"Excuse me!" I rolled my head and blinked my eyes hard as fuck before I looked down at the bag of Tom's Salt and Vinegar chips and the Dr. Pepper that I had in my hand.

He gave me a half smile and moved out of my way.

"Thank you," I said as I glared at him with caution. I was wondering why the fuck he was fucking with me when I didn't even know him like that. I'd never seen this mixed man a day in my life, and Slade would cut the fuckin fool if he found out that I was out here talking to and entertaining another nigga in his city.

I turned around and looked back at him after I placed my items down on the counter. He was just standing there at the set of double doors where people could walk in and out of the store. Our eyes connected and then he opened the door to leave. I felt an uneasy feeling wash over me, and I couldn't help but wonder what that was all about. Did he know me or something?

"Girl, I know that look. He likes you." Britin stood to the right of me at the counter smirking.

I couldn't take my eyes off her as she looked up out the glass of the store door.

"Yeah, but I don't like him. Slade will kill me and that man." I took my change from the cashier and grabbed the black store bag. "Thank you," I told the cashier.

"Fuck Slade. That nigga cheatin on you with bitches all over the city anyway. All he gon do is pacify you with money and material things."

My friend telling me shit like that about my nigga was like a punch to the face. She ain't know shit about our relationship nor why I chose to stay with him even though I knew that he was creeping 'round on me with this bitch and that bitch. Maybe I liked the money, maybe I liked the material things, and maybe it was just the dick that kept me around. I can't pinpoint what it was about Slade and me, but I knew that I was in love with him, and I was staying regardless of what Britin had to say about our relationship.

"Let it go Brit!" I said through gritted teeth, because I didn't wanna hear nothing else about my man.

"Naw, you need to hear this. All yo dumb ass gon do is take it like a lil kid in a candy store," she said, downing me, and telling me how she really felt about me.

This bitch, I though in my head. "Well bitch! I'm glad to know how you really feel about me. So, I'm dumb Brit? That's how you really feel?"

"You always run back to him. It doesn't matter what he say or what he do to you. You always playing fucking stupid for him. Courtney. Stop flexin! Bitch, you'll stop breathing if that nigga asked you to."

4

"He takes care of me! And for the record bitch, we broke up," I told my friend.

"Whoop-de-fuckin-doo!" Britin said.

I tossed my bag in the driver seat of my car, unscrewed the gas top to my gas tank and glared at her.

Britin stood there in front of the passenger door, clapping her hands, and looking down on me.

"It's too damn bad that y'all gon be back together soon," she said. She looked away from me and in the direction of the niggas that had just pulled up to parkin' lot pimp and flex in front of the store. "Excuse me! Sir! Sir, come here," she said to the man that had stopped in front of me in the store.

I pursed my lips together and started to tell her to stop, but he was already walking in our direction. I didn't have the demeanor to make a scene in front of all these people, and if Slade caught wind that I was acting out in public, he'd fuss at me about how it made him look like his bitch was out here handling shit that he should've been handling. That's what I loved the most about him. He didn't fucking play about me, period.

"My friend's newly single. She needs a new distraction. Well, she needs a new man in all seriousness. Can she have your number?" Britin asked this good-looking ass man.

"Why don't your friend ask me?" he asked without taking his eyes off me.

"Because, I'm not interested," I raised my eyebrow at him.

"Good, cause I wanted you to have my number anyway. Give me yo phone."

Britin had already opened the passenger door to grab my phone out of the cup holder and hand it to him before I could put up a fight or protest.

"I hate you," I told her after I finished pumping the gas

and after she'd given him my phone number to this man and called him on my shit.

"You just gon be hatin me then," she said.

We went to the hood where we posted up and flexed hard as fuck in front of all the hood bitches that were either baby mamas or pot head ass hoes. Most of the women that were out on the block didn't want more for themselves other than the attention of the dope boys and petty ass drug dealers that were either thieving or in and out of the correction system. But me; I wanted something different.

ONE WEEK Later

This nigga was always blowing my shit up, tryna come wherever I was at, and calling me just so he could listen to the noise in the background, but I always answered my phone whenever he called me. Today was a little different, though, cause Slade didn't call me before he came knocking on my door like he was the fucking police. We were laying on top of the comforter set of my bed when he grabbed my phone that was sitting in between us.

"Gimme that back!" I jumped up and reached my right hand up in the air to try to take my phone away from him.

"Why you reacting like that? Huh?" he asked me. I sat on top of my knees and looked up at him like a puppy. "You usually let me go through yo shit! Why is it a problem all of a sudden?" his voice boomed throughout my bedroom. He now had wrinkles in the center of his forehead from the frown that he was wearing on his face.

"Cause Slade. It ain't like we go together, and you ain't my nigga no more! Just give it back!" I whined. He huffed at me and pushed me backwards on my bed. "Damn!" I smacked.

Slade stood in the center of my bedroom looking at the picture that was on my lock screen before he looked up at me.

"What's the password?" he asked me.

I turned my head to look away from him, but I knew better than to play with him and not answer him when he asked me something. We'd end up fussing, fucking, and fighting whenever I made him ask me shit twice, so I drew in a sharp breath. I twisted my lips to one side of my face and contemplated lying to him.

"It's 54753," I told him.

He unlocked my phone and stood there going through my shit. I was more than confident that he wasn't going to find anything in my phone, cause I didn't get caught doing my dirt and shit. I knew how to play a nigga, so I kept two phones with me. One for my main nigga, and the other one for people that I dealt with whenever I felt like dealing with them. Plus, my secondary phone would go dead, and Slade had the number to that bitch, but he never went through it. I always kept it turned off and hidden from him. I looked up and felt my phone smacking me on the side of my face before I knew it. I didn't even think to grab the side of my cheek. Instead, I looked directly at him. I was anticipating him to jump on me at any given minute.

"Wha-What you do that for Paiton?" I asked him as I called him by his government name.

"I should've fucked yo girl Britin when she tried to throw that cat at me, but nawl. I thought you were the one for me. You always showing me that you can't stay down and be loyal to a nigga."

"Slade, fuck you," I told him.

"Nah, bitch. FUCK YOU! Stupid ass hoe," he said before the muscles in his arms flexed.

"That's how you really feel Slade? Really?" I jumped up from my bed and ran over to stand in front of him.

"Ion even know why I keep fuckin witcho ass," he said as he poked his index finger in the center of my chest while he talked to me.

Slade pushed past me and walked out of my bedroom. I ran behind him, but my apartment door just slammed in my face, in front of me. I couldn't believe this nigga. I had no clue what the fuck I'd done for him to treat me like this. Britin was right; I was his fool and I'd definitely stop breathing if he'd asked me to, but what did he just say to me? He should've fucked my friend when she tried to throw that cat at him. I snatched open my apartment door and looked at him as he smoothly walked away from me.

"SLADE! SLADE! GET BACK HERE!" I yelled and screamed before I realized that he didn't give a fuck about me or the way that I was feeling. "What the fuck did I do?" I asked myself aloud as I closed the door and walked to my bedroom to flop down on top of my comforter. I searched through my phone to figure out what he'd seen that caused him to act the way that he was acting towards me.

2

Adric

Damn, I just couldn't stop thinking about her. The cute ass girl that I'd seen in the store; she wasn't star struck or thirsty like these other hoes were for me. Shit, I found myself asking myself all week, "Does she know who the fuck I am?" Either she didn't know who I was, or she just didn't give a fuck that I was that nigga in the city. I had her number, but she also had mines, and she hadn't tried to text me or call me, yet. I wasn't bout to put myself out there and hit her up first. Fuck alla that. One thing Adric

Hernandez never did was sweat a hoe. I kept it playa, and I was too playa for all of that shit. I could tell that she was into someone else. Hell, I was sitting here wondering if she was taken by some other nigga. That shit had me in my feelings cause I couldn't stop my mind from wondering about her.

I was damn near running myself crazy tryna figure out where she was at and worrying if she was okay wherever she was at. I couldn't help myself because I felt an instant attraction to her like she was a hotspot or a WIFI connection or something. I looked around at the niggas that I rarely chilled with on the block and asked them about lil mama cause she was bad as fuck and I had to have her for myself.

"Aye y'all! You remember that girl that was at the store? Any of y'all know her name or anything about her?" I looked around in everybody's face and waited for someone to speak up first.

"Damn man, you must be really tryna hit that?" Devin asked me.

I shook my head from side to side before I said anything back to him. "Tryna get to know her. It's much deeper than sex," I confessed to him and all them niggas that was surrounding us.

"Oh, ggggaaawwwwddd!" he said and a few of them other niggas chimed in right with him.

"Gone on with that. But, do you know anything about her? Where can I find her? Where she be at?"

"Nah. Ion know nothing. I just know that she's Slade's girl."

"Mmhuh. What's her name?" I asked him.

"Her name is Courtney. Courtney Adams, I think," Devin answered me.

He had all these niggas looking at me like I was crazy

or some shit cause I was feignin for this chick.

"You ever see her over here?"

"Nah, nah! She might slide through every now and then wit her friend, but he keeps her cooped up in the house or either she be at work workin' or some shit. Say they've been rockin for a while now. That's the one that he keeps to himself. That's the way to his heart. You wanna get back at that nigga Slade, then fuck with ha," he told me.

"He loves her like that?" I frowned up my face and looked around the hood as if I wasn't the least bit concerned while I waited for him to answer my question.

"That's his most prized possession my nigga."

"Fuck!" I rubbed my right hand along the bottom of my chin and started to get mad at myself for falling for this chick.

I knew all about Slade. the nigga's a hustler just like me, and we both get money, but shorty ain't even look the part to be the girlfriend of a plug let alone the connect. I raised my right hand over my forehead to block the sun out of my eyes and then I started thinking of ways that I could get close to this girl again. I wanted to, nah! I had to see her again.

My name is Adric "AD" Hernandez, and I'm a thirty-three-year-old connect out of Puerto Rico. I'm a mixed breed, coming from an African American and Puerto Rican bloodline. I'm a tall, skinny ass nigga with short, black, silky hair, and I work out a lot too. I went to Morehouse College and majored in software engineering. I had a pretty laid back, chill type of job, so I had to occupy my time with doing something else on the slow days at work. I chose to follow in my cousins' footsteps by hustling on the side, and I'd become damn good at it, so I kept on trapping.

Trapping soon turned me into one of the hottest connects to run Atlanta. Now, I don't have to stand on the block from sunup to sundown, 'cause I got street runners moving dope and cooking up that work for me. Most people would never think of me as being that nigga that was running shit here in the city cause I kept it casual and simple, so I knew the reason why Courtney hadn't made my phone jump yet. She probably thought that I was a lame ass nigga that was driving my homeboy's car, but she couldn't have thought that. It was apparent that she wasn't paying attention to all the ice that I had on me the day that we met.

"Aight. I'mma holla at y'all later," I told them niggas before I started dappin' them up and bumpin' shoulders with a few of my soldiers and lieutenants.

I was walking away from my crew when a few of them girls from the hood came running towards me. I tried my best to hide the expression that I wanted to wear on my face, 'cause I ain' want them hoes to think that I was looking down on them, but they couldn't bag a nigga even if they had their hair did and was wearing a fresh new outfit. There was this one girl that was feeling me outta the group, but she was afraid to step to me, so she had her lil clique walk her over to me. That shit ain't impress me. If anything, it made me feel like shorty was insecure, and plus, she wasn't my type of bitch anyway. I stopped and smiled at them before I gave the woman that was the ring-leader of the group a lil talk time, but I already knew what she wanted.

"What up ma?" I asked her.

"AD, I was wondering if I could get yo phone number," she said to me before she turned around to look at her friends. I waited for her to turn around and look at me, so I could shut her down real quick.

It wasn't the fact that she wasn't worth it, but I didn't want her; I wanted the girl that made my mind wander. The girl that had me chasing after her. Shit, whoever this Courtney chick was , she had a nigga head fucked up.

"I'm good on that Rachael," I told her. I made sure that I used her name to let her know that I knew her name and to try to put a bandage on her bruised ego. She was a bad lil vibe in the 'jects, but still… I couldn't stop thinking bout that one.

"Ugh! What you mean? You good?… You good?" she asked me.

I could tell that she was surprised that I'd turned her down. I mean, what nigga wouldn't want to hit one of the baddest bitches that came up out of the projects. Rachael didn't have a bad reputation or nothing, but at the same time, my mind and heart wanted who and what it wanted.

I held my head down and shook it, because it was hard dissing her like that in front of her friends, but I just couldn't give her my number like that. I ain' want shorty to be blowin' my shit up.

"Yeah, I'm good on that. I'll see you around."

I couldn't even give her a half smile or nothin' cause I ain' wanna be that nigga. I ain't wanna hurt her more than I'd already done by turning her down and denying her the chance to get to know a nigga. I felt guilty all the way home, but I was reminded once I pulled into my driveway that I had everything I wanted, except her.

I started conjuring up ways and coming up with clever plans to get to Courtney Adams again. All I wanted was to just be in her presence again. I knew that all I had to do was swallow my pride and call her myself or pop up on her while she was with her man to let her know who the fuck I was and that I wanted her all to myself. I wasn't gon stop until I got what I wanted.

3

Britin

Damn, that nigga Adric was over here. Shit, he wasn't dressed like he was a boss, but you could tell by the way that them other dudes on the block was showing love to him that he was somebody with that check on him. I couldn't stop staring at him and the other dudes that were sitting on top of their cars or standing with their arms folded across their chests. Some of these niggas had money and I was looking for a baller to move me up out of the projects.

It didn't make no damn sense that I was twenty-four years old, still living in my mama's three-bedroom, government assistance apartment, yet I graduated from an HBCU as a marketing editor. I got a job and all of that, but still I loved balling out and splurging my money on my bundles, nails, and Fashion Nova outfits and shit. You know, I had to look like money even if I ain't have it.

All the niggas look at me and I turn heads cause I'm a Texas bred woman, but I moved to Atlanta with my mama after my father was gunned down for resisting arrest. He and his baby mama had got to fighting, and he knocked her ass out for disrespecting my mama. I was too young to understand any of that, so I just tell everybody that I'm from Atlanta whenever somebody ask me where I'm from. Shit, I've lived here since I was seven or eight years old, so I don't remember much about Texas other than that whatever I was drinking in the water down there had filled my thick thighs and hips out. I even have the size 36C cup breasts to match my voluptuous ass. I was standing here watching Adric dap up everybody and this Rachael hoe and her crew walk up on him.

"Gah-damn!" I said to myself.

Rachael was my only competition in the streets of Hotlanta cause she was damn near as bad as I was. I knew that she was going to have him wrapped around her finger in no time, 'cause she was always pulling niggas. Whether you'd see them together or not was the kicker. I only learned about the niggas that fucked with Rachael after she was through with them. I sucked my teeth and a smile grew on my face once I saw her and her crew look at each other like they were shocked or hurt or something.

Mmhmm. Good for her ass, I thought in my head.

I stood there looking on wishing that AD had of stopped in front of me at the convenient store instead of stopping in front of Courtney's entitled ass. It wasn't like she was all that. Hell, she was a smooth seven and I was a good eight if it came down to looks and shit, 'cause at the end of the day, we were just girls from around the way. I second guessed myself and my ability to pull him cause I knew that my girl was gon be trippin if she found out that I went behind her and took a man off her hands that was interested in her.

"Damn, she always getting the finest of the bossed-up niggas. Niggas always choosing her when she don't even be paying them no attention or showing them no interest," I mumbled as I walked towards my mama's apartment.

I thought about stopping Adric to ask him if he'd heard from my friend, so I turned around and walked back in his direction, but the closer that I got to him, the more that I could tell that something was bothering him. He looked mad as hell, so I left well enough alone even though I had a good feeling that Courtney would curve him for Slade. I pulled my phone out of my back pocket and called him, Slade.

"Yo! Britin. Why da fuck you ain't tell a nigga what was going on? Why you ain't tell me that Court was talkin' to my connect. Yo! Yo! Naw! Ion wanna hear none of that cappin shit that you got to say to me. I just wanna know why you ain't tell me," he fussed as soon as he answered his phone.

I removed my phone from my ear to look at it and make sure that he was really going in on me and that I'd called the right person, and then I placed the phone back to my ear.

"Slade! Hol' up! Slade!"

"Bring yo ass to my house!" he yelled through the speaker.

"And what type of friend would I be if I came over to

your house now that you and Courtney are on the outs? You know how y'all do. Y'all forever getting back together and fuckin each other on the low. I'm not finna be no quick nut for you to throw up in my girl's face the first time that you get mad at her," I told him.

I listened to the silence on the other end of the phone line and reminisced on Slade and me.

"I should've chosen you Brit. I should've put you first. I made a mistake by getting with her because of her pretty ass face."

"Ion wanna hear that shit. Bye." I felt the hurt in my chest when he confessed that shit to me, 'cause I really didn't give a fuck about what he should've did. What he did spoke volumes to me, so what he was gonna have to do was more than tell me what he should've motherfuckin did in the beginning. Fuck him.

"Just come through. I promise. You won't regret it. I won't," he started.

I was five seconds from blacking out on his ass and telling him how the fuck I really felt about him tryna check me for not telling him what his slut ass bitch was out here doing, and then he had the nerve to ask me to fall through to fuck with him. I think the fuck not! Shit, these niggas was always trying it. Tryna have their cake and eat it, too, but he had the right one. I removed my phone from my ear again and stood in front of my mama's screen door, tapping my foot on the porch, and waiting for him to continue telling me what he won't do to me.

"I won't disappoint you, ever," he told me.

For a second, he touched me. A little piece of my heart turned soft for the nigga, but naw. Slade was in love with Courtney, 'cause he always got back with her. Always, and nobody could ever figure out what type of hold she had on him. All these bitches hated Courtney cause she bagged

Slade even though the whole hood knew that the nigga wasn't shit. He ain't give a fuck about nothing that he did or who he got caught with.

"You love her?" I asked him, sounding all insecure, and getting in my feelings for him for a hot lil minute.

"Yeah, but you got a nigga heart though."

I rolled my eyes and tried my best not to cry on the phone with him. I choked up, so I grabbed the handle of the screen door, and took a few steps inside of my mama's apartment.

"And if I'd of fallen for that shit Slade? Boy, bye! Get off my line! Yo playa ass almost got me," I told him through my fake chuckle and laughter.

A bitch was hurt and all that I wanted to do was hurt him or go in my room and cry in my pillow cause I was sad and lonely.

"You comin or what?" Slade asked me.

I could tell that he was irritated, but I had to know. I wanted to know what the hell he was calling me for. Oh, now he wanted me.

"What you calling me for?" I retaliated.

"When and how did Court meet that nigga Adric? I sucked my jaws in together and jerked my head back because I just knew that I couldn't be hearing him correctly.

"Oh, so that's what you calling me for? That's what you wanna know?"

I was rolling my eyes up at the ceiling because he was really tripping. I couldn't believe that he had the audacity to call me asking me questions about his bitch and some other nigga. I wanted him to want me. Why was I being overlooked? What was the fuck wrong with me? Shit, the last time we fucked, Slade was talking big shit and telling me how he was gonna leave Courtney to be with me. He said that he loved this pussy.

"Tell me. Come over," he moaned into the phone.

I almost melted where I was standing when I heard him moan that shit to me cause I was in love with my best friend's man. He was a big drug dealer and his pockets were swollen with dough too. I knew it was wrong, but I just couldn't get enough of him.

"I ccccaaannn'ttt!" I whined on the phone.

I felt the wetness drip inside of my panties cause I had been holding out and waiting on him to fuck me again. It felt good to hear him say that he wanted me, but I didn't want Slade to just pick and choose when he wanted to fuck with me. I knew to keep a baller ass nigga, you had to give them something that them other bitches weren't giving them and that was attention. Bitches always frolicked to him, but me. I was trying my hardest to make him need me. I wanted to be like the high that he needed after a hard day at work. "You know that she doesn't deserve this shit. No matter how bad I want you Slade," I told him.

"Man, bye. Call me when you stop worrying bout these other bitches. Yeah, she my girl or whatever, but who the fuck am I fucking? Who am I tryna fuck? You, so you better act like you know," he said before he hung up the phone in my face.

Slade and I had only fucked one time, but I swear it was the greatest sex that I'd ever had. We were fucking like we'd done it more than once. It was the best because wasn't nothing new with us. Shit was the bomb, but I'd been denying him every time that he called me for sex. He was not about to treat me like I was second place or some leftovers after dinner. The fact that he got back with Courtney had turned my heart cold cause I expected the sex to make him forget all about her, but she was where he wanted to be at. I drew in a sharp breath and slowly walked to my bedroom to close the door and lock it behind myself. I did the only thing that I could do, cry myself to sleep, and wish that I'd never fucked that nigga.

I hated my best friend because she always got to live the life that she deserved, and she was always the chosen one when it came down to bagging a good, paid ass nigga.

4

Paiton "Slade"

Going through my baby's shit and seeing her entertain another nigga had me in my feelings. I couldn't believe that shorty would try and play me like that. After all of them times that I took that bitch back and curved her friend. Yeah, a nigga slipped up. I fucked on Britin one time when me and Courtney had broken up, but shit I kept coming back to her young ass, so that should've told her what was up wit us, but nah! Shorty ain't never see shit my way. She couldn't see the love that a nigga had for her. She wasn't dumb; she was just blind to the shit. Maybe a slap in the face from her phone would wake her the fuck up cause she had me feeling like Plies.

She could play stupid and give me away if she wanted to. That was gon be on her, but I knew what my lil head was telling me to do. I was gon call Britin to check her bout not giving a nigga a heads up and get her to slide through, so I could slide up inside of her wet tight coochie. Man, Britin made a nigga feel like taking off the rubber with her and leaving passion marks all over her neck, but Courtney. Man, Courtney's fuck faces and the way her pussy lips gripped my dick made me always wanna look at her when I was digging deep inside of her pussy.

I'd sped home, enraged. I was ready to cut ties with this motherfuckin nigga Adric Hernandez.

"Not my bitch!" I screamed as I pounded my fists against my steering wheel.

I ain' give a fuck what she did or how much money she spent. Long as Courtney didn't give my pussy away to another nigga, she and I would forever be straight. She was always on that sneaky shit and I couldn't stand it, but I couldn't deny the way that she had a nigga. I was like a sick puppy for her. My basic instinct was to drink whenever I was heartbroken or I felt let down by someone, so I didn't hesitate to pour up once I parked my car in front of my four-bedroom house. I poured some brown Jose Cuervo inside of a red SOLO cup and drank two shots straight to the head before I popped open a can of Seagram's ginger ale to mix inside of a third a cup of liquor. My throat and chest burned from taking my shots straight with no chaser, so I put a few ice cubes inside of the cup and tried to numb the feeling of betrayal that was deep inside of my heart. My main bitch was always dogging me out, but at the end of the day, she was the only woman that my heart truly fuckin wanted.

"The fuck she let me catch her texting other niggas in her phone for!" I fussed aloud to no one in particular.

I couldn't handle that shit. The fuck shit that Courtney was on when it came down to us, she made it hard for a nigga to trust her. I needed for Britin to pick up and tell me what the fuck was going on with my bitch and my connect. Hell, the plug wasn't good enough for her. She had to go and get with the connect. So, Courtney wanted a big fish ass nigga. Well, I was gon get her back and fuck her best friend, again. I know that Britin had told me that she wasn't tryna go there with me, but I wasn't an average ass nigga, so I figured that she was somewhere crying cause of my confession to her. I sipped on my drink and pressed her contact ID to call her back to try and talk her into coming over to the crib to let me hit that.

"Mmm," she moaned into the receiver.

"Baby, what you doing? You sleep?"

"Something like that," Britin said all nonchalant and shit. I knew that she was just frontin and putting on like she was mad with me.

"I need you right now. Come and see me. Please," I begged her.

"Ugh, Paiton." I loved it when she called me by my first name. "Alright, I'm on the way," she told me before the phone went silent against the side of my face.

A big smile spread across my face because this was my last chance to let her know how I felt about her.

My name is Paiton "Slade" Perez. I'm twenty-nine years old, Hispanic, and I'm real fit with a six pack to match. I'm a paid ass nigga to only be a high school graduate. Shit, I wanted to go to college, but my pops had other plans for my life. I find myself envying my lil bro, Khari

Perez cause he gets to live out his dreams, playing soccer, and achieving a secondary education.

I've been doin this hustling shit since I was nineteen, so it wasn't much a motherfucker could tell me about moving muscle and pushing dope. Our family was a part of the cartel, but I wasn't ever comfortable with taking orders and being a motherfucking worker.

I took a shower and told myself that I was gon holla at my lil bro after Britin came through and I got rid of her. My doorbell rang as soon as I was stepping out my shower, so I wrapped the bottom half of my body in a towel and ran downstairs to answer the door. It couldn't have been nobody showing up announced like that at my crib except Britin. She was looking good as fuck when I snatched the door open, so a nigga didn't waste no time pushing her up against the wall in my foyer and digging up inside of her. We ended up on my bed upstairs, cuddled up like we were a couple, pillow talking and shit like we usually did. She always looked me in my eyes when I talked to her. I ain' gon lie, that shit made a nigga have a soft spot for her, and it made me feel like I was special to somebody. I felt like someone wanted to hear me out and listen to me. The girl was good at making me feel like she genuinely cared, but still I couldn't stop myself from hurting her. It damn near killed me to see her crying tears.

"Fuck! You know how much I love Courtney. Brit, what you expect a nigga to do?" I asked her.

"Stop getting back with her! Stop going back," she said through her tears.

"It ain't that easy Britin." I ran my right hand up and down my forehead and face cause I couldn't just up and leave Courtney for Britin.

They were fucking best friends and I wasn't trying to hurt Courtney in the end. I didn't want to hurt Britin either cause what she and I had was real, yet I had to take responsibility and be a fucking man. Courtney was a safe choice and it was easier for me to be with her than if I'd gotten into a relationship with Britin because Britin was a liability and she was the type of bitch that would fuck some shit up if I didn't give her what she wanted.

"Damn, is she that much better than me. My head game and pussy must ain't good enough for you?" she started.

"God damn girl! This what you wanted?" I rolled over on top of her and lifted the both of her legs over my shoulders, so I could feast on her as if she was a buffet. "Huh?" I bit down hard into her thighs and then I licked the spot where I'd bit her at and placed soft kisses up and down her thighs and legs.

I loved the way that the girl ran her hands up and down my head when I was going down on her. Britin wasn't like these other bitches. She ain't wrap her legs around me and make me feel like she was tryna keep me pried in between her legs. She knew how to keep them legs up, so I ate the fuck out of her pussy, played with her ass and made her suck my fingers while I pleased her.

"Ion want the sex. I just want you. I just want you!" she cried out as she came all over my face.

I looked up at her with her juices running down my chin with a puppy dog look on my face cause I wanted her to forgive me for the way that I was making her feel. Britin leaned forward towards me to kiss and suck her juices off my face. My shit got back rock hard again, so I pushed her back and fucked her like she was the one that I was in love with. We took turns competing with the other to see who was going to get tired first, but I wasn't giving in. It was wrong as fuck what I was doing, but I couldn't stop pinning her hands down to the bed to make her look me in my eyes as I fucked her until I made her cry. She had to see it; she had to know where a nigga's heart was at, but I just couldn't give up what I had going on right now. I'm a selfish ass nigga, but I was willing to be the one that changed her mind about me.

"I love you Britin," I confessed to her.

"I love you too," she sniffled through the tears that I was making her cry.

Britin and I were wrapped up for thirty minutes before I asked her if she was ready to dip and get up out of my shit. She looked at me like she was surprised, but I had to be mean to her even when I didn't want to be. I was in love with the girl, but I was her best friend's man. I prayed that she'd forgive me and that we could work it out and be together in the end of all of this, but for right now, I had to get rid of her and handle my business.

Britin took that shit like a G. Like it didn't even faze her and got dressed without so much of saying anything hurtful to me. I tried my best to stall her cause I ain't really want her to leave like that, but I could sense that she was really done with me. I stood up and walked her out, but she didn't tell me that she loved me or ask me for a hug before she left me this time. I felt like I was losing her, but my hands were tied and there wasn't much that I could do to make it better between us.

"FUCK!" I yelled after she pulled out of my driveway.

I slammed the house door behind me and walked towards my brother's room to see if he was home or not. I knocked on his door, but I didn't wait for his ass to answer it because this was my house, and I didn't need permission to go inside any room inside my crib. I saw this fine ass dark-skinned chick pull the covers up towards her neck.

"What up lil bro? You got school today? Or you ready to get down wit yo big bruh?" I asked him.

26

Khari jumped up from the bed and ran over to his room door to push me out of his bedroom. I laughed a menacing laugh and listened as the lock on the door turned. He could quit with that embarrassed ass shit cause I was bout to hit that lil bitch that he'd just hit soon as she walked up outta there from being with him. I started up the staircase when I heard a loud knock on my front door.

"I know this ain't 12!" I said aloud as I turned around to walk down my stairs and answer it.

5

Khari

I was cheating on my girl with this chick named Mya that I'd met in the club a few weeks ago. I wasn't expecting my older bro to come knocking on my room door. It seemed like the nigga knew when I had company or something. My conscience knew that it was wrong for me to lay up in the bed with this girl and bask in the after-sex glow, but my girl was blowing up my phone, and I wasn't in the mood to deal with her nagging and shit. Daisha and I had been seeing each other for the past year, but we were always arguing cause she complained that I didn't spend enough time with her.

My phone vibrated against my dresser, but I ignored it cause I knew that it couldn't have been nobody else but her. Damn, I loved my girl, but I just couldn't be faithful to her.

I'm Khari Perez and I'm the baby boy of the Perez Cartel Organization, but I ain't getting involved in that drug dealing shit cause I'm a lame ass nigga that would rather work for every dollar that I get. Hell, the president already tryna deport my people anyway, so I'd rather take my chances by doing things the right way than bringing attention to myself and fucking over my damn self.

My father's in Cuba right now, making alliances, and being stingy with his money because he wants me to drop out of school to come and work for him. I keep telling him that it's important if someone in our family graduates from college with a bachelors or master's degree in something to benefit the family operation, but I know that he knows that I'm just selling him the false hope that I'll come and work the family business.

I pride myself on being smart, but I wasn't smarter than my father, Kapri "KP" Perez. I'm eighteen years old and I work the floor and front desk of a fitness center here in Atlanta. My job is to seduce the older women and the young girls to make them sign up for a gym membership and visit more often. My off white, tan skin tone complemented my muscular physique and benefited me getting the job at the fitness center.

I got up from my bed and walked over to my dresser to read the message from my girlfriend, Daisha. Daisha was always in her feelings and insecure when it came down to trusting a nigga, so I always read her messages and responded back in a timely manner to keep her from popping off or popping up on me with the bullshit. Even though I was fucking around on her, I knew not to play with Daisha cause she was crazy as hell and that shit turned me on about her. It scared the fuck out of me, but crazy was good, and I loved her attitude the most. I was shocked when I picked up my phone and read the message from my bro.

Big Bro: Aye bro. Let me hit that lil bitch when u finished wit ha.

I had to re-read the message again to make sure that my brother had sent that disrespectful ass shit to my phone like that. We had never shared bitches before, so this shit was new as fuck to me and I wasn't wit it.

"Fuck!" I said to myself because if he was tryna hit a bitch that wasn't my main bitch, then I knew that he'd try Daisha when I wasn't around and shit.

"Aye man! Get up. You gots to go," I told Mya before I knew it.

I had to call my bitch and tell her not to come through when I wasn't home cause my bro had me looking at him sideways. "I hope she ain't still with this clown ass nigga," I said aloud.

"Huh? Who you talkin' bout? And why I gotta go? It ain't like I been over here that long witcha. Oh, you gotta check in witcho girl. Fuck ha," Mya said.

She was getting under my skin cause she was tryna play a role that she didn't have the credentials for. Hell, I wasn't even too much into my own bitch anymore, but still, I wasn't going to let her disrespect her. I snapped my head around and looked at her like she'd said something about my mama or something.

"Don't say shit else about her again," I warned her. "Stay in your lane and play yo role hoe," I told her before I knew it.

I left her standing there with her mouth wide open and opened my room door, so she could leave out my house.

"Oh my God! I don't even know why I gave you the pussy and let you hit it. Don't nobody even want you but Daisha anyway. Y'all deserve each other. Don't ever call me again!" Mya yelled.

"Hoe, you just mad cause you gave me yo loose ass pussy and I checked you for disrespecting my girl. You think just cause we fucked that you special or that you hold some type of rank or something? Girl, get the fuck out my shit!" I looked out the door and into the hallway before I turned my head to widen my eyes at her as a sign for her to hurry up and move around.

"UGH!" she scuffed before she brushed past me to leave out of my room.

I followed behind her towards the house door and noticed Slade standing there talking to my girl.

"Man, what the fuck? What y'all two got to talk about?" I asked Slade.

"And who is this?" Daisha asked me with a roll of her eyes and neck.

I watched her talk with her hands and point at Mya with an attitude. Damn, she was gonna kill me if she found out that I'd fucked Mya in my room. I stood there frozen, feeling guilty, and too afraid to tell her the truth.

6

Daisha

I'd been calling Khari's phone all day because I wanted to know what he was wearing on our date, so that I could match with him. He didn't answer the phone earlier, so I assumed that he was at the gym. The time that we were supposed to meet had done came and went. His phone was just ringing until the voicemail picked up when I called him, so at first, I waited for him to call me back. I got dressed in the outfit that I'd picked out to wear on our date after two hours had passed. Khari had tried this shit with me once before, so it was funny that he was trying me again. I let it slide the first time as a courtesy because he was fine as shit and I really liked him. The fact that he was standing me up once again showed me that he didn't give a fuck about me.

I ain't even know why we were still in this relationship when he was talking about going off to college in a month anyway. I felt like I was wasting my time with him, but the nigga had money, and all the hoes wanted him, so I had to keep what I had bagged already cause I ain't want nobody else to have him. The more that I called him, and he ignored my calls, the angrier I became because at times he'd make me feel like I was unimportant to him. The thought of him being with that bitch really set me off because he'd always say that she was nothing to him.

"*She's sis,*" he'd tell me whenever I asked him why he was spending so much time with her.

"He betta not have his ass up under Courtney!" I screamed as I jacked my lip gloss applicator inside of the MAC lip gloss tube.

"Don't go over to that boy's house doing no crazy shit!" My auntie told me.

"I'mma fuck that mansion up if he got ahn otha bitch over there! I'm tired of him telling me that Courtney's his brother girl cause hell… she's always with him. Auntie, somethin bout that don't add up. Something ain't right bout that, but I'mma find out what the fuck they got goin on. I be damned if this nigga gon fuck around behind my back like I'm some fool or something. Who is this bitch to him?"

"Baby, calm down," she tried reasoning with me.

"Uh! Uhn! I'm finna go and see what's up. I been calling this nigga's phone all day. I don't know who the fuck he think he playin!" I stormed out the front door and walked to my car like I was running away from somebody.

"Daisha! Daisha! Don't do nothing stupid!" My aunt Jackie warned me.

"I'mma burn that bitch down if he playin with me!" I screamed loud enough for her to hear.

I was listening to all kinds of heartbreak music and dialing his phone while I was on my way over there. The shit was still ringing till the voicemail picked up, so I knew what the fuck was going on. I was ten seconds from nutting up, so I pressed my right foot down harder on the gas pedal to do 90 miles per hour all the way there. He had me fucked up cause we didn't miss no phone calls from each other.

Now if it had of been me not answering the phone, Khari would've been childish and put me on the blocklist for a couple of days. Oh, he wanted to play, I could play. His ass better not had another bitch in there when I got there. I reached over into my dashboard to see if I had my gun with me, so I could pop his ass if he was doing it like that. My feelings were hurt because we had a date today and he went MIA on me out of nowhere. She must've been pretty special to him to make him forget about our plans. I pulled up in the driveway and couldn't make out who the car belonged to that was parked behind his.

"The fuck!?" I asked myself.

I pushed my gearshift forward and listened to the sound that it made when I stripped the gears. My anger was getting the best of me, but I didn't have to go inside of the house to know what the fuck was up. The bitch's car was parked behind his, so that told it all right there. Whoever this hoe was followed the nigga to his crib, but I had something for the both of their asses.

"Aww, hell no! Hell to the fuckin nawl!" I said aloud as

I stepped out of my car to walk around to this black 2016 Toyota Camry.

I read the numbers on the tag and pressed my forehead up against the windows of the car to look inside and figure out if this car belonged to a female or a male. The tint was a little dark, but I could see the Carmex, lotion, and feminine items inside of the car. My temperature was rising, and I had to get inside to find out if this female was with my man or with Slade's hoe ass, so I walked around the house to look through the windows. I tried to open the doors of the house, but they were locked, so there was nothing else that I could do except for knock on the front door. I took my time walking back around the front of the house cause I ain't want to react as soon as the door opened and seem as if I was a maniac. My hands reacted for me when I balled my fist up and pounded them against the French doors.

"Bam! Bam! Bam!" my fist knocked. "OPEN THIS DAMN DOOR!" I screamed. "WHERE THE FUCK HE AT?" I yelled to Slade once he came to answer the door.

Slade grabbed me by my shoulders to stop me from walking in the direction of Khari's bedroom.

"Calm down. Bae, bro sleep," he said to me.

I rolled my tongue against my front two teeth, smacked my lips together, and then I twisted my lips to the opposite side of my face to let him know that I didn't believe a word that he was saying to me. I almost fell for the shit until a female came walking up the hallway from the direction of Khari's room, and then he came following behind her. My heart was crushed, and I felt so motherfucking stupid for even coming through unannounced on some surprise shit.

"And who is this?" I waved my index finger as I talked.

My head and neck were rolling. I rolled my eyes after Khari acted stupid like he ain't hear me, so I asked him a-motherfucking-gain. Maybe the bitch would speak the fuck up and answer me.

"Who the fuck is this bitch?" I asked Khari.

"I'm Mya bitch!" she said to me.

Khari turned his back to me and took off in the direction of his bedroom. I ignored Mya because she couldn't have meant much to him cause he ain't say shit to defend her or try to take up for her when I asked him who the fuck she was to him. I followed behind Khari and tried to open his room door, but the cheating ass dog had locked it.

"Pussy ass nigga!" I screamed behind the door. "Open this motherfuckin door Khari! I'll kick this bitch down or, better yet, I'll throw a chair through this motherfucker!" I yelled.

"Man, just go away!" he screamed back at me from behind the door.

I hated how he did his dirt and pretended like I was wrong for catching him in the act. That shit broke my heart and made me feel like he never wanted to be with me in the first place. If he loved me, then why was he cheating on me? I'd just forgiven him for the same shit, but his family had money, and I wasn't trying to give him up, so another bitch could reap the benefits of all the coaching that I'd given to him.

I made him believe that he was worthy of a woman's love and I built his confidence up when he didn't believe in himself. I was there for him all those times when he called himself bad names and contemplated committing suicide. I'm the bitch that talked him out of killing himself, on some real shit. My knees buckled beneath me and I used the palm of my hands to hold onto his room door as I broke down crying in front of his brother and the woman that I'd caught him cheating on me with.

It frustrated me how he pushed me away from him and

how he acted like a child instead of a grown ass man. He was wrong, dead wrong, and I wasn't going to keep letting the shit slide and burying the hatchet like it was okay. Obviously, Khari had gotten used to stepping on me like I was a doormat. I sat there crying in front of his bedroom door, too embarrassed to look behind me to face his brother and Mya. I begged him to let me inside of his room. I heard the volume of his TV grow louder from inside of the room. I couldn't hurt any worse than I already was hurting, so I cried hysterically once I noticed that he was trying his best to tune me out.

"I ain' got time for this shit!" Mya said with an attitude from behind me.

"Yeah, you need to dip," Slade told her.

I felt someone's hands touch me on my shoulders, but I figured that it couldn't have been anyone else other than Slade. I slightly turned my head around to my left to look behind me and raised my eyebrows at him. Khari and I were both young as hell, so I couldn't say that we knew what love was or if we were even ready for a serious relationship, but I'd tried my hardest to protect my heart from situations like this.

"Don't cry. Ssshhh! Let me dry your tears. C'mon." I sniffled and wiped the tears that were falling down my cheek with the back of my hand.

Paiton used his hands and pulled me up by my armpits, so that I was standing up on my feet, facing him. I closed my eyes and cried because I was so ashamed and mad at myself for crying over his fuck ass brother in front of him. My mouth dropped open in amazement when his hands slid down inside of the front of my shorts. I couldn't believe that Khari's brother was fingering me right outside of his bedroom door. My eyes shot open and I noticed Slade looking down in my face when I looked up at him. I covered my mouth with both of my hands to stop myself from moaning out loud in front of his doorway, and then I tossed my head back to allow the pleasure to overtake my pain. Slade removed his hand out of my panties and pried my hands away from my mouth, so that he could insert his fingers in between my lips.

"Come on," he whispered to me.

I licked his fingers and followed him to his bedroom. Slade waited for me to walk inside of his bedroom in front of him before he closed and locked his bedroom door behind us. I felt his dick press up against my ass after he'd turned off his bedroom light. The feeling of nervousness washed over me because I knew what was about to happen between us. He covered me in his arms and started unbuttoning the button on my shorts as he kissed me along my neck. I couldn't help myself, so I moaned his name out loud because he was making me feel wanted. He pushed himself into me until I fell face forward on the bed and then he used the tip of his dick to play with my pussy lips before he made the wetness from my secretion smack against my pussy lips. I bit down on the cover of his bed in anticipation of him entering inside of me. I felt my body move forward onto his bed and then I let out a shriek.

"Ugh!" I gasped.

"Take this dick," he said to me. Slade bit down on the side of my earlobe and then he kissed me along my neck as he intertwined his hands inside of mine and pushed deeper inside of me on the bed.

"Ooohhh Slade! Don't-Don't stop fucking me!" I screamed as he pumped his dick in and out of me.

He rolled me over and looked me in my eyes as we sexed each other, but I quickly turned my head away from him.

"This dick made you stop crying?" he asked me, but I

didn't say anything to him. He lowered himself on top of my chest until we were chest to chest, and then he turned his head towards mines, so that we were eye to eye. "Answer me," he moaned inside of my mouth.

"Yes," I whispered to him.

"Damn, you got some good ass pussy," he confessed to me.

"Slade, stop! STOP! Mmmm!" I moaned out as I looked him deep into his eyes.

"You want me to stop? That's what you want?"

"Keep going! Don't stop. Oooohhh, ugh! Slade! KEEP GOING!" I grinded my hips and rolled them into a circular motion before I wrapped my arms around his neck to throw this pussy back at him.

"Let me have it," he said.

"It's yours," I promised.

7

Idris

"Damn, where the hell you at Mya?" I looked at the call log on my phone screen.

I started to worry the more that I called her and got no response. I tried to call her once more, but now her phone was going straight to voicemail. I exhaled a sigh of frustration and grabbed my car keys off the counter. I left the apartment and made a run to the corner store to grab a pack of Swisher Sweets to smoke the stress away from missing her. I kept trying to call Mya on my way to the store and finally her phone was powered back on by the time that I left the store. She still wasn't answering any of my calls.

I drove in the direction of her mama's house instead of going back home cause I was worried sick about my shawty. Mya and I hadn't been together that long cause everything had moved so fast between us. I never thought that I'd fall in love with a woman that had a significant age difference than me, but Mya made me change my mind.

I parked along the curbside in front of Mya's mama's house and sat there rolling up two fat ass blunts. I didn't fire em' up, 'cause I didn't want to be high in front of her mom like that. Even though I was a stoner, I chose to have some respect for her mother in hopes that she'd have respect for my family and my mother. Mya's mother told me that she hadn't talked to or seen her daughter today, so my anxiety shot through the roof. I didn't know if something had happened to her or if she was okay, but I needed to know something. I thanked her mother and then I drove home, smoking on that kill, and trying to Facetime my girl to make sure that she was straight.

"FUCK! FUCK! FUCK!" I yelled when her Facetime voicemail picked up. I stopped by the convenient store to grab another pack of cigarillos.

I purchased another packet of Swishers and drove to the hood to chill with my niggas instead of sitting at home, thinking, and worrying about my girl. My eyes were heavy from smoking so much weed and I was high as fuck by the time that I pulled up to the hood. I grabbed my Ziploc full of Captain America OG sativa and the foil of cigarillos to go and post up on the block with my niggas until Mya called me back. My boys were keeping me occupied, but I kept checking my phone, wanting my girl to just hit me up to let me know that she was okay.

I looked up to see Britin walking in our direction, so I sparked up a blunt of sativa and appreciated the body that she was serving. She walked right over to where I stood and pushed up on me to let me know that she wanted me. I gave her a half smile and looked up to see Mya briskly walking over towards us.

"Aww hell!" I muttered loud enough for Britin and my boys to hear me.

"You remember me from the store?" Britin asked me.

"Yeah, I wanted your ass then, but you were acting all silly. You weren't paying a nigga no attention. Now, I'm taken and my girls on the way over here," I said to her as soon as Mya stopped alongside us.

"Uhm!" she started as she looked back and forth in between the two of us. "What the fuck is going on over here?" Mya stepped in between me and Britin.

She was ready to set it off about her man.

"I've been calling you bae," I told Mya.

Mya looked at me, smacked her lips, and then she diverted her attention back to Britin.

"I suggest you make room for I make change with your ass. Idris's my man! You can have any other nigga round this group, but this one. This one right here belongs to me. K?" Mya asked Britin for reassurance or as if she was speaking to a person with special needs.

"Or what hoe?"

"Smack!" Mya had done punched this girl in her mouth.

I shook my head, laughed, and pulled her off Britin. "Why you ain't been answering your phone? You'n need to be worried bout these other bitches. Leave that girl 'lone. Come here baby." I rubbed her along her arm and pulled her inside of my chest. "You had me worried boutcha. You know daddy love ya," I said to her.

42

"Why you got these hoes all up in yo face?" Mya asked me.

"Yo, where you been at all day?" I pulled her back from inside of my chest, so I could look her in her face.

"Just handling some business," she told me, but I could tell when she was lying to me, and I couldn't stand that shit.

"Meet me at the house." I walked away from her cause I let her get away with too much and Mya was going to keep lying to me if I didn't check her bout the lil petty shit and put her back in her place.

I wasn't that nigga for her to run over or play with, so I had to let her know that I knew her like the back of my hand. She wasn't gon like the shit, but I was gon try her soon as we got to the house, and if she denied me of fuckin her, then I was gonna know something was up. I'd been sitting at home, blowing her phone up all day, and then she had the nerve to come to the hood with that fighting shit all cause a bitch was tryna get at me. I had to smoke on the way home to shake the thought of the game that Mya thought that she was running on me. It was gonna be a wrap for us if she'd been out fucking on another nigga behind my back.

I parked my car behind hers and tried to touch her as she walked up to the door, but she tensed up on me. *Um huh!* I said to myself. I grabbed her by her neck and gently slammed her back up against the door before I tongue kissed her.

"Where the fuck you been at all day girl?" I asked her in between kisses.

"I was-I was out," she mumbled beneath me.

I lifted her chin up and stared deeply into her eyes. "Let me find out you been lying to me." I groped and touched all over her body.

43

"Don't even start with that shit," Mya smirked at me before she broke away from my embrace.

"Where you going bae?"

"I need to go and bathe. Damn, Idris. You was just smiling in some other woman's face and you wanna try and flip the script on me like I'm the one that's wrong. I've been out all day. I'm sweaty baby," she laughed, but I wasn't falling for that shit.

"Aight, go and get the water ready. I'mma be in there to join you in a second."

"Uh ughn baby! I just wanna bathe by myself," she said, confirming my suspicion, and making me wanna rip them clothes off her skin to sniff her skin for some other man's scent.

"Cool, cool." I walked in the opposite direction and went and took my shower in the spare bathroom.

I finished washing my balls and laid there in the bed with my dick up in the air as I waited for her to walk out of the bathroom. Mya had on her grandma night gown, so I knew that she was bound to turn me down when I initiated sex between us tonight. I watched her walk over to the bed and ignore me and my hard dick. She climbed in the bed with me and turned her back to me to scroll up and down her Instagram newsfeed. I pulled the covers back and scooted my body close behind hers before I wrapped my arms around her small frame.

"Ugh, baby not tonight," she moaned.

"Hush girl and stop playing wit me," I whispered as I nibbled on her ear.

She swatted her hand up in the air to shoo me away. I could sense that she'd been out doing some slick shit. My bitch was fucking on another nigga and coming home to lay up with me.

"You gon give me some pussy?" I asked her again.

"Ugh uhn. I'm not in the mood for all that. Why we can't just kick it and watch TV Idris. I mean damn. We got plenty of time to fuck. You stay all up in my shit anyway, so I don't know what you trippin for," Mya turned around and said to me.

"Alright then bae. I feel where you coming from. Let me take the stress up off you and eat the pussy then." I was trying her to see if she was gon turn down the head cause you know that women loved to get their pussy ate on the regular.

"Idris! No! I just wanna go to bed."

I could see the deceit in her eyes, so I did what any nigga in his right mind would do.

"Yo, get the fuck up and pack up all yo shit. I want you out of here! You've been out cheatin and think you finna come home and lay up wit me. Man, you buggin. I ain' never even thought about stepping out on you. I stay curving bitches on the strength and you gon repay me like this. I don't want nothing else to do with you. Get the fuck up and go Mya! Go. I wish I never met you."

A nigga hopped up out the bed heartbroken cause I didn't let these women get me this deep in my feelings. I was a savage ass nigga before I met her, and I'd let my guard down just for this chick to play me like I was an average ass nigga.

8

Jeremiah

I'd been chilling in my homeboy's room, watching the basketball game on TV, and listening to his lil bro's bitch cry and go off on them downstairs. I was sitting in a chair in his room with the lights turned off, so I could see the game in HD. That shit had me feeling like I was sitting courtside at the game in person. I saw Khari's girl walk inside of Slade's room first, and then I noticed my dawg walk in his room behind her with his dick pressed up against her back. Damn, he was bout to take his bro girl down right there in front of me.

My dick rose in my pants at the thought of watching it all go down. I unzipped my pants, pulled my dick out of the slit of my boxers, and rubbed my hand up and down my shit until it got rock hard in my hands.

I bit down on my bottom lip to stop myself from screaming shit as I listened to the smacking sounds of her pussy lips. Ssshhhiiiddd! I was ready to beg Slade to stop teasing her with the tip of his dick cause I could hear the sounds of her pussy juices smacking against the skin of his dick. I was ready to get up outta the chair and join in with them. I heard lil shawty let out a squeal and then my nigga fucked the bitch from the back until he turned her over and put her legs up in the air. Them motherfuckers were in their making love, but that wasn't my business. I was just tryna bust a nut and get up off that shit real quick, but as soon as I was bout to bust the doorbell rang. I started beating my dick real quick and was hoping like fuck that Slade and Daisha didn't hear my hand clapping up against my shit. I grunted and got up from the chair to go and see who the hell was ringing the doorbell. I tucked my dick back inside of my pants and forgot to zip the zipper before I answered the door to let her in.

"Whaddup Courtney? Slade know you over here?" I looked behind me at the staircase nervously before I turned back around to face her.

"You think I'mma just show up at his house unannounced?" she asked me.

I was thinking of a lie to tell her, so that I could stop her from coming in, but she kept on talking to me.

"I mean, I could if I wanted. Since he is my nigga. Or would that be a problem witchu?" her smart ass asked me.

"Aye, don't try me with the bullshit. You know a nigga

only fuckin on a bad bitch. If yeen belong to my partna, then I'd bless you wit this dope dick, but you can't handle this dick lil baby," I told her naïve ass.

She ain't need to be with a nigga like Slade cause all he was gon do was manipulate her. She was young and dumb, and he'd trained her to be at his beck and call. It amazed me how much she loved him no matter the wrong that he'd done, but she was bout to find out the fuck shit that he was on.

"Boy stop! Where Slade got his ass at?" Courtney giggled and showed off the dimple in the left side of her cheek.

"He's upstairs." I pointed at the staircase behind us and smirked a knowing smirk cause I was bout to burst her bubble and watch her flip the script on him.

I followed her fine ass up the steps and wished that I'd have one chance to fuck the shit out of the girl cause she was bad as hell. Any nigga would've wanted to trap Courtney with a baby. She killed the game with her personality alone, but the whole hood knew how intelligent she was. She'd gotten with Slade and tossed her dreams into the crab barrel with the rest of the bitches that he kept on his team. We stopped in front of his room door, and I watched her gasp when she heard the moans that were coming from the other woman. I waited for her to say something and for her to turn up on Slade or Daisha about what she was seeing, but she was weak. Her shoulders fell up and down as she cried in the doorway of his bedroom, and then Slade turned to see where the crying noise was coming from.

"How could you? HOW COULD YOU DO THIS TO ME?" she questioned him.

Slade climbed up off the bed and walked over to where Courtney stood then wrapped his arms around her.

"GET OFF OF ME! YOU GOT YO DICK ALL OUT. YEEN EVEN WRAP IT UP WITH THAT BITCH. FUCK YOU SLADE! FUCK YOU! But you tripping on me," she cried.

I stood there watching them like I was watching a soap opera.

"Aye boss, you want me to get her out of here?" I pointed to Daisha, his brother's girlfriend.

Courtney barged on inside of his room, and then she turned her head to look at Slade like he was crazy.

"I-I know the lights are off, but is this Khari's bitch? You fuckin on your brother's bitch? You did all this to get back at me?" Courtney started walking towards Daisha, but Slade grabbed her and picked her up.

"I want you. I want the both of y'all. Fuck, just let me fuck," he kissed her and placed her down on her back. "Daisha, come eat her pussy while I talk to my girl," he demanded. Daisha looked at him and crawled down to the foot of the bed to go down on Courtney without hesitation, so I walked back over to the chair that I was sitting in to finish getting off.

"Um. No, no! MMMmmmm! Yes. Tssss. Shit! That's fucked up Slade. Ugh! Yyyyeeesss!" Courtney moaned and screamed.

I couldn't help myself. I had to get up and join in. I stood there behind Daisha, touching on, and groping on her. I didn't want that bitch; I wanted Courtney. I wanted to fuck her real good and bust my nut off in her. She was a trophy bitch and Slade didn't appreciate her and he damn sure didn't know what to do with her. Slade stopped kissing on and feeding Courtney lies to demand the women switch positions. He told Daisha to sit on his face while he fucked Courtney. I stood there in the darkness beating my meat and holding back my cum. Slade got up and told the women that he'd be back.

"Aye man! Follow me downstairs. I'mma let you get in on this action," he told me.

We went into his kitchen and fixed four cups of lean and grabbed the ecstasy, then we took the cups and drugs back up to his room.

"You sure bout this? We gon make this a four-some?" I asked my mans.

"Yeah, just wrap that shit up and don't nut in my main bitch," he told me.

I nodded my head at him and thought to myself, "*This motherfuckin nigga stupid if he think I ain' finna get her for myself. I'mma bust in her every chance that I get.*"

We gave the women the cups of lean and talked them into taking the e-pills, and then I joined in to fuck Daisha until Slade got jealous. I'd heard their chemistry earlier, so I knew that he was feeling something for her especially since he wasn't strapping up with her. He was fuckin on his brother's girl without protection, so why should I respect his bitch, especially when she was all that a nigga wanted? I dragged Courtney's tight, wet pussy and came all up in her shit before she realized what I'd done and started yelling out for Slade.

"My bad. I had to make sure that you'd be in my life forever. I been wanting you for a long ass time. Don't abort my baby," I said as I kissed her all over her face and neck.

I kept stroking my soft dick inside of her pussy to make sure that I was pushing my nut deeper inside of her cervix.

"Is you crazy?" she asked me.

"Man, get up off my bitch nigga. Nigga, I told you to strap up with her. I told you not to nut in my...I know you didn't. Aye holmes. I just know you didn't!" Slade fussed at me.

"Fuck nigga. Yo bitch wasn't off limits just cause you said that shit. I been wanting to get Courtney pregnant before you got wit her. She betta not abort my kid," I told him and her.

"GET UP OUTTA MY SHIT!" he started swinging on me, so I got dressed, and left his house happy as hell cause I'd fucked on his bitch and came all up inside of her.

A nigga was bout to be a daddy if she kept my seed for me. I wasn't an ugly ass nigga or nothing, but most women overlooked me cause I stayed to myself. I'm a weirdo, crazy as hell, and I'm considered a geek or a nerd, but that was just fine with me.

I got inside of my car and drove home, geeked, and ready to share the news with my mother that I was finally giving her a grandchild. My friendship with Paiton was no longer, but it was worth it to have the woman in my life that I always wanted. I'd had my eyes on Courtney since she was in high school and knew that she deserved more than what she settled for. I wasn't stopping until she got what she deserved and made something out of herself. The love that I had for her was real, but she had to want to love me back and give a nigga a real chance. I wasn't the man that she thought that she knew based off our interactions when it came down to her man. Slade didn't give a damn about her cause if he did, then he wouldn't have allowed me to fuck her.

Courtney would've never given me a chance if I had of shot my shot with her and I've always wanted her to be my baby mama, but I knew that she'd never fuck me either, so I did the only thing that I could do and that was to trap her.

Yeah, a nigga switched roles with these bitches and did what they'd usually do to their niggas, but I'd been in love with the girl since I first seen her. I promised myself that

51

I'd leave her alone for the next couple of months to see if she'd choose to keep my child if I'd succeeded in getting her pregnant, and if I didn't then I'd convince her to let me hit that shit raw again. I got off the phone with my mama, took a shower, and prayed that God would answer my prayers and bless me with a child with my dream girl.

9

Mya

I rolled out of bed confused cause I couldn't understand why Idris was tripping on me just cause I didn't want to have sex with him. There was no way that he could've known what I'd been out doing, but his actions made it seem like he knew. I wanted to give in to him and let him slide up inside of me, but Khari wasn't a lil dick nigga and my baby Idris was packing. I wouldn't be able to grip his shit and then he'd know for sure that I'd been giving his pussy away. I just, I just couldn't take the dick cause it would bring me more pain than it would pleasure.

I stood there in his room, lost and confused, cause I didn't know if he was serious about me leaving. Idris was staring at me like he was furious, and I didn't want to come clean to tell him where I'd been, but I knew for a fact why he was trippin on me. It was because I'd turned off my phone while I was fucking on another nigga.

"So, you kickin me out cause I don't wanna fuck?"

"Nah, I'm asking you to leave because you're lying to me."

"About what?" I asked him.

"I know you better than you think I know you. Mya, you're being dishonest with me about something, but I can't allow you to break my heart, so I want you out of my house since you can't come clean wit yo nigga. You my girl and you won't even fuck me on the regular, so that alone tells me that either you been out fuckin or you got something and you're too scared to fuck on me."

"No, no! Where am I supposed to go?" I asked him.

Everything in me was screaming, just fuck the nigga to keep him and shut him up, but I couldn't bring myself to do it because my shit was sore as fuck.

"How much you need for a room? You must can't go back to yo mama crib?"

I couldn't believe that the man that I was once head over heels in love with was dogging me like this and talking to me crazy. He had me ready to go upside his mother-fuckin head, but I couldn't bring myself to do it because I was the one that was out fucking and cheating on him. Idris is a good man, but he's always busy and working. He ain't never satisfying me in the bedroom, and then he wanna wait till I done went and fulfilled my needs and taken care of my craving to wanna try and have sex with me. I stood there hurt cause I wasn't tryna leave him or give him up. Even though I was doing my thing, he belonged to me and he was still my man. My lips were quivering as I tried my best to hold my emotions in.

"Idris! Don't do this to me. I don't wanna. I don't wanna go. I wanna stay here with you. Baby wait, hold up!" I followed behind him.

I grabbed him by his wrist to stop him from walking away from me. "I'm not lying to you about nothing. I'm just tired tonight. I haven't done anything," I continued lying to him.

He stared inside my eyes, but I couldn't help but to turn my head to look away from him.

"See, it's that shit right there. I can tell when you're lying to me!" he yelled. "Girl, I done studied you. I know you better than you could ever imagine. I want you to leave. Right now!"

I was at a loss for words, and I didn't know what to say to him, but I damn sure didn't want to move back in with my mama cause we didn't get along. When I got with him everybody in my family looked at me like I'd hit the jack-pot. This was going to hurt them more than it was hurting me. I felt like he was waiting for me to cry some more and beg to stay with him just so that I wouldn't have to move back in with my mother, but shit… I wasn't that bitch.

I turned around and walked back in the direction of his bedroom to start removing my clothes out the dresser and started packing up my shit. I heard him snatch up his car keys before I heard his house door slam. A part of me wanted to stay while the other part of me knew that he was for real and that he wanted me to be gone by the time he got back. I packed and cried before I called my mom to see if I could move back in with her.

I'm a great catch and I could be a great woman to any

man, but I needed affection, time, and attention. Idris was always getting his money and I respected that about him, but still; I needed him to act like he wanted this shit. I could tell by the way that that he was acting that he wasn't fucking nobody else, but me. Yet and still, all the material things that he bought to put a smile on my face didn't mean shit when he wasn't laying up in the bed beside me. That shit made me feel insecure, like he was with someone else, and like I wasn't good enough for him.

My name is Mya Davis, I'm twenty years old, and I loved fucking with older men cause they know how to treat a bitch. My mannerism, grace, and elegance are what made Idris take me out to dinner and move me in with him. He wanted me to be in the house when he came home from work, so I moved in with him without thinking twice about it. Now, I'd fucked up a good thing by fucking round, but I'd rather have my sanity than go insane behind a nigga that I was tryna keep. I sniffled the tears and tossed things inside of my duffel bag before my mama continued talking to me.

"Baby, there ain't no way that y'all can work it out? Idris is a GREAT man, and he has money," my mom emphasized on the phone to me.

That's what hurt me the most with her; she and everyone else in my family thought that he was so great. He barely even spent time with me, and all he ever wanted to do was go to work and chill with his niggas. I felt like he was more into them than me, but this one time that I told him no, he asked me to leave.

"Ma, money ain't everything and if he's so great then why would he ask me to leave?"

"Well, what did you do? You pushed him away! It had to be you. That man's crazy bout you," she continued belittling me and making me feel like I was always the problem when it came to me and him.

"I did what any bitch in her right mind would do when a nigga told her to leave. I packed my shit and left instead of staying with him."

"Mya, I'm still your mother. You need to watch your mouth and respect me. You need to make it work with him."

"Ugh uhn ma!" I cried.

"Well then, come home then daughter," my mother said before she hung up the phone in my face.

I knew that she was mad at me for having to come home, but she would get over it. Money wasn't everything, and I shouldn't have cheated on Idris, but if he knew that I was cheating on him, then why didn't he say something? I looked around his house one last time and wished that we could've spent the rest of our lives in bliss with one another, but we lacked communication and trust.

10

Courtney

I couldn't believe that Slade would even let me get fucked up to the point that I was fucking his homeboy, Jeremiah. The sex was good, so I couldn't complain about that, but what turned me off was Jeremiah coming inside of me. I didn't know him like that and he damn sure didn't know me.

I jumped up off Slade's bed once I realized that semen was dripping down my inner thighs and I became disgusted. I ran out of Slade's house with Slade right behind. I pressed the unlock button on my key ring, got inside of my car, and pressed the lock button to lock the doors. He stood outside beating on my driver window, pleading with me to tell him what had went on, and looking at me concerned as shit.

"He nutted inside of me! How could you do that? How could you share me with your friend?" I screamed hysterically.

I placed my head on my steering wheel and cried like a baby because loving Slade was mentally draining me and hurting me to my core.

"Bae, I'mma get that nigga for what he did to you!" he yelled to me.

I started up the ignition of my car and replayed the night over in my head. I turned the radio off and cried during my drive home cause I felt like I'd been violated even though the sex was consensual between Jeremiah and me. I just wanted to get home and take a bath to get the sperm off me. I was disgusted because I didn't want to end up pregnant with this nigga's baby.

"I JUST WANT TO GET IT OUT OF ME!" I screamed as I drove in silence.

I rushed inside of my apartment and ran to the bathroom, so that I could sit on the toilet and push the nut out of my vagina.

I sat there thinking about how I ended up in this predicament in the first place. This nigga was always calling me to come through whenever he was on the bullshit. I swear, it seemed like sometimes he just wanted me to be there with him. Paiton wanted to spend every second of the day with me, but when I wanted to spend time like that with him, then he was busy. His excuse was always either he had to go hit a lick or make a play. Tonight, was no different. He was trippin cause I wasn't at his house, in his bed, waiting up on him, or blowing his phone up like I usually did. I was mad as hell when I walked in Slade's bedroom and saw him fucking another bitch especially since I'd done something that I never really did before. I popped up at his house to surprise him since he was complaining about me not being there for him.

"The nerve of this nigga," I said in my head as I cried from the hurt and betrayal.

He was always cheating on me and making me look like a damn fool for staying with him and continuously loving him. I usually wasn't down with none of his antics, but things had been rocky between us and I thought I'd never admit that he was my first love. I was down for him no matter what, so I was willing to do any and everything to make him happy with me. My thoughts started racing, and I'd convinced myself that a threesome was what we needed to make things right between us, so I shut the fuck up and allowed him to please me. I'd always wanted to be a mother, but I didn't expect for shit to go down the way that they did tonight. Now, I'm sitting here on this toilet, mad as hell cause the dick was good and Jeremiah wasn't a bad catch either, but he was a weird ass nigga. I wasn't tryna get pregnant by him or have his baby cause the father of my child was going to have to be a nigga with big bags and big bills. I didn't want my baby to ever want for nothing.

I strained and pushed out as much of Jeremiah's cum as I could push out of me, and then I took a shower. I put on a pair of comfortable pajamas and then I climbed inside of my queen-sized bed. Tears streamed down the side of my cheeks as I reminisced on the sex that I shared with him and cried myself to sleep.

The following morning, I picked up my phone and noticed that Slade had called my phone at least ten times throughout the night. I had my sounds turned off, so I missed all of them calls. I turned my sounds to vibrate and scrolled through my call log when I accidently pressed AD's contact ID. My phone automatically called him. I hurriedly pressed my index finger down on the red end button on my phone screen to hang it up, but the nigga was already calling me back. I turned my phone face down on my bed, but I could still feel the vibration from the incoming call, so I answered to see what he wanted.

"Uh, hello. My bad, I didn't mean to call you," I told him.

"Damn. I wanted to hear your voice again. Let me see you."

I rolled my eyes up in my head cause he sounded just like these other niggas. Niggas was always tryna come through and see a bitch, but I was going through some shit. It was early in the morning, so I was surprised that he was up and that he'd called me back so quickly.

"I um. I had a rough night." I groaned and stretched in the bed before I sat up and placed my back against the headboard.

"Where you at?" Adric asked me.

"I'm at. I'm at home, umm," I started before he cut me off to say something.

"Text me yo address and have on something real comfortable. I'm on my way as soon as you send me the addy," he said to me.

I frowned up my face, removed the phone from my ear, and looked at my phone screen.

"Wwwwhhhaaatttt?" I asked myself aloud before I watched the timer on my phone screen flash.

11

Paiton

"GOD DAMN IT!" I punched a hole in the wall of my foyer and listened to Daisha's voice as she talked to someone upstairs.

The bitch had me feeling like Ronald Isley as I walked up the stairs inside of my house. *I know she ain't talking to herself?* I asked myself. I opened my bedroom door to find her on the phone, but I noticed that Daisha had my phone in her hand once I got closer to her.

"Who was you in here talking to?" I snapped.

"How you gon fuck me and have me telling you that the pussy yours, but you got bitches calling your phone?" she asked me.

"Aye! You my bruddah bitch, not mine. Don't be answering my shit. Gimme my phone bitch!"

"Here. Slade, you know I don't love him, but I've gotta know. Who the hell is Britin? Daisha sat up in my bed and groggily asked me.

"Look, you can take your ass to sleep or go back home shawty," I told her.

"Do you love her? Your girlfriend?"

I ran my hands over my head and huffed, but she just kept on laying it on thick.

"I'm all yours now. I promise." Daisha looked at me nervously like she was waiting for a confirmation from me.

"We broke up. That ain't my girl. Fall back lil shawty cause I ain' tryna fall. You still belong to my bro though. I just wanted to dry your tears."

"Keep that shit playa, huh?" She asked me before she rolled over on her side and turned her back to me.

I was furious, but I didn't want to say nothing out of the way to Daisha cause I knew how I'd fucked her earlier and she had every reason to be in her feelings. I turned around and walked out my room to go to my kitchen and pour myself up something to sip. I was in between Hennessey and Crown Apple, so I stuck to the Crown cause that Hennessey would put me in the mood to fuck and I wasn't tryna fuck lil baby head up. It was wrong for me to fuck on my brother's hoe, but she was bad as fuck. Plus, he'd already gotten caught cheating anyway. I went out the back door of my kitchen and sat outside in a lawn chair, right in front of the pool, and scrolled through my social media accounts on my phone. I couldn't stop thinkin bout Courtney and if this nigga had done followed her home, so I called her phone. All kinds of crazy thoughts were going through my head when she didn't answer the phone.

"She bet not be wit no other nigga," I said to myself before I downed the last lil bit of Crown Apple that was sitting in my cup, mixed with ginger ale. "That nigga Adric Hernandez," I said.

I went upstairs, took a shower, brushed my teeth, and cuddled up next to a bitch that I barely even knew. I woke up and snuck inside of my office to try calling Courtney again. My head was fucked up over her, so I dismissed my brother's girl and got fresh to hit the hood. She complained about how she wasn't ready to go and tried to seduce me into dicking her down again, but it was prime time for me to get this money. I didn't have to hit the streets and work the trap, but I wasn't going to tell her that. She had to go. It was five o'clock in the morning and them first, third, and fifteenth checks had done hit, so I needed every bit of the money that she had me missing.

I got rid of Daisha and sped over to the projects to check every block that I had my workers working. It seemed that the only way that I could get my mind off Courtney was if I was busy doing something or working. Courtney wasn't even my girl no more, but she knew what it was wit us. Shit was always gonna be forever when it came down to me and her. I dapped up a couple of niggas. I was proud that they were out here on the corner putting in this work, but I was frustrated with my bitch. She wasn't supposed to ever fall for the bullshit cause she was headstrong and would always tell me no when I came to her with the bullshit.

"Y'all seen that nigga Jeremiah?" The muscles in my jaws flexed when I mentioned the fuck nigga's name.

Shit, I was fucked up when I chose to let him hit my

bitch. I didn't usually ever bring Court around none of my niggas. The closest that they came to seeing her was either in the club when she was standing right in front of me or on her social media profiles and shit.

"Nah, naw. We ain' seen him," one of my workers answered.

"Aight, good cause that nigga ain' welcomed over here in my hood no more." My voice was stern because I meant what I said.

I looked around the block and thought about the woman that had my heart from the start. I was waiting on them niggas to ask me why I'd banned Jeremiah from coming to the hood, but they knew not to ask me no questions about what the fuck I'd just said to them. I continued checking on the movement of my product and collecting my dope money from my street runners and my lil soldiers.

"Aight boss," a few of them young bucks said to me.

"You see that nigga AD ova this way today?" I asked my lieutenant Justin.

"Man say, that motherfuckin nigga can't stop askin bout Courtney. I'mma have to hit that myself to see what she talkin' bout," he said to me.

I drew back and punched that nigga in his jaw before I knew it. Shit, a nigga just lost his temper. I ain' mean for shit to get out of hand like that, but she was my only weakness when it came down to the things that I loved. I loved the bitch like I loved a new car and I couldn't help but to be possessive over her.

"FIGHT!" the hoodlums yelled out before people from the hood came running to try and break us up.

It was dam near six o'clock in the morning and I was out here fighting wit niggas over some pussy that I wasn't even getting no more. My partners broke us up and I stormed off into the direction of my car, so I could pop up on Courtney. I'd only fucked with my brother's girl because I thought that she wasn't going to come through and see me, but when she came I was down with the threesome once she chose to participate. In the back of my head, I knew that she was doing it because of me, because she wanted to keep me happy. I hated it when she did shit to please me and to keep me in her good graces. I always wanted her to be that bitch that told me no and challenge me to level up in life.

I popped a pill and smoked a blunt on my way over to Courtney's apartment, but something wasn't right. I knew shorty and she normally would call me back and answer my calls by the third ring. She never kept me waiting for long and she'd drop any nigga she was with for me, so I broke into her apartment once she didn't answer her phone.

What I saw set me the fuck off. Here my bitch was, lying next to Adric "AD" Hernandez, sleeping like a baby, and making me untuck my burner. I breathed heavily and pointed my gun at the two of them before I reached for my phone to turn my sounds off. I loved the fuck outta this hoe and she always seemed to play the fuck outta me. She knew exactly what to do and how to get under my skin. Courtney was the only woman that could hurt me dawg. I sat down in the computer chair that sat in front of the desk that was in her bedroom. I watched him hold her while she slept and then he stirred in his sleep.

"Yeah, get up. Gone head and wake up pussy nigga," I said to myself.

He stretched and admired her facial features before he placed kisses all over her face while she slept. My blood was boiling like grits that boiled on a pot on top of a stove. AD touched her body and then he checked his phone before he pulled her closer into his chest and nuzzled his face in the crevice of her neck. I sat there watching him with the woman that I'd loved despite her turning her back on me when I needed her in my life the most. I couldn't believe that this nigga was doing all the things for her that I never took the time to do. It hurt like hell to watch another man love the woman that I saw myself having a future with, but I wasn't putting my gun down though. I was going to wait for them to wake up and realize that I was there because I was ready to kill them both. If I couldn't have Courtney, then no one else would. I'd kill her before I watched another man love her.

12

Adric

I was nervous as fuck when I called Courtney back cause she hung up before she gave the phone time to ring. I was hoping that she wasn't calling me by accident because I'd been waiting to hear from her. All I needed was to hear her voice. I wasted no time jumping inside of the shower and finding me something to wear. It was early in the morning and I usually didn't go chill with hoes during booty call hours. I checked my phone after I got out the shower and noticed that she'd came through for the kid and sent me the addy. I hurriedly placed my shoes on each foot and grabbed my house keys, so I could fall through and see what she had going on this time of morning.

I parked my car outside of her apartment building and gave myself a pep talk before I got out to walk up to her front door. A nigga was scared as hell cause I didn't know her like that, but I made that choice to go to her crib. I tapped my fist against her door and waited for her to answer the door and let me in.

"Hey," she said as she stepped back.

I couldn't help but stare at her figure as she stood with her body leaning up against the side of the door.

"What's up shorty? You ain't got nobody else in here with you, do you?" I looked around the apartment suspiciously to make sure that she wasn't tryna set me up and to be for sure that she wasn't on no slick shit.

I heard a smack come from her lips, so I turned around to see if she'd caught an attitude just that quick.

"Naw Adric. Ain't nobody else in here with me. My room's this way," Courtney pointed as she stood on the side of me.

A man of my caliber couldn't get caught slippin with a hoe ass trick, so I had to peep shorty and figure her out a little bit. Courtney was different from all these other bitches cause even though she knew she was the shit, she was humble with it. I was intrigued by the way that she dressed, basic, and how she preserved herself. It was like she had the blueprint on how to make a rich nigga want her and go out of his way for her. I can't lie, she was the baddest, so you could see why a nigga would want to drop a bag or two on her. My head was spinning cause I was tryna figure out what I was finna do with her lil ass. I wanted to fuck the shit out of her so bad, yet I knew that she expecting that from a nigga. I had to show her that I was different than her boyfriend, Slade. Hell, I was the nigga in the city and all these bitches were wishing that they had the chance to meet me. Couldn't no bitch pull me.

"Aight, aight. Cool," I said as I watched her hips move towards the entrance of her bedroom. *Fuck! Damn!* I said in my head.

I cupped my hands around my dick to cover up my dick print and then I flopped down on her bed. I had to do something, so I made myself comfortable, but I could tell by the way that she was moving around her room that something was wrong with her. The scent inside of her apartment made me feel like I was at home already and I didn't want to leave her. *Already*, I thought to myself. Shit, I had to figure out what she and I were bout to do cause she had me feeling a way that no other woman had made me feel. Courtney had me looking at her and contemplating calling my mama to let her know that I'd finally found the one. Yeah, the connection was that strong.

"Um," she started before she turned around to face me.

"You can leave the lights on," I told her.

"I'd rather not," she whispered before she flipped the switch and came over to join me in her bed.

"Chill shawty. What's wrong witchu? I can tell something's on your mind. You aight?" I rubbed my hand up and down her arm to comfort her,

I tried my best to get her to relax and calm down.

"I-I um. I um, I went over Slade's house last night," Courtney started that crying shit.

She broke down in front of me and I couldn't help but want to help her out in some way or another, so I pulled her close to me.

"I gotchu. What happened?" I asked her.

I felt a fire ignite deep down inside of me for my shawty. I couldn't stand this feeling. I couldn't stand it cause I knew that from first sight, shorty had me.

"I did a threesome with him, that turned into a four some with his friend Jeremiah. And he, and he…Jeremiah came inside of me! I don't want to! I've always wanted to be a mother, but not like this. Not like this!" she placed her face inside of the palms of her hands and cried.

I watched in amazement as her shoulders heaved up and down. I was astonished, so I couldn't say nothing. My mind was boggled because I knew every woman had a bit of freak in them, but Courtney. She was undercover with the shit and I was with it, but I could tell that she was hurting. I couldn't be the one to put her through no more pain, so even though I had every intention of fucking the bitch; I had to refrain from taking it there with her. I'd heard her correctly. I'd heard her when she told me that her man's best friend had came inside of her. Man, that shit frustrated me cause she had to learn how to use protection no matter how close she thought she was with a nigga. Men would raw dog any and everything if you let them, but I was like her. I was different.

I rubbed her on her thigh and stroked her arms while she cried inside of my chest, then I pulled her back, so that I could stare at her face.

"Did you hear what I said to you?" I asked her.

Courtney just looked at me like she was spaced out or something. Her face had tear streaks on them, and her eyelids were puffy. She was so fucking beautiful to me, even when she was crying. It was like she was the girl of my dreams and all I could think about was a little girl that resembled her facial features. She was, she was perfect to me. I wanted to make the girl my everything, but first I had to get rid of Slade and now this nigga Jeremiah. I'd heard about him, but he was no competition. I knew how to get up under his skin if Courtney ended up with his seed, and that was by raising and loving his kid like it was my own.

"Huh? What? What did you say to me?" she asked me. Courtney continued talking before I could answer her question. "I'm sorry that I'm crying like this. I should've never. I was trying to delete your number out of my phone when it called you this morning. I didn't mean to call you. I didn't mean to call. I'm so-." I stopped her from talking and apologizing to me by covering her mouth with my lips.

"I said, I got you," I reminded her of what I'd said to her and I could tell that it frightened the hell out of the girl.

She sucked in a bunch of air and returned the kiss as I watched the tears fall from her eyes onto my lips. I licked her salty tears and continued kissing her like I'd never see her again. By now, I was lying on my back with her on top of me. My infatuation with Courtney was getting the best of me since she'd just told me that she was being careless with the men that she chose to have sex with. I wanted to strip her out of the clothes that she had on and fuck her problems away, but I just couldn't. I couldn't take it there with her cause another man had been bussin up inside of her.

"Thank you," she said to me before I helped her get off top of me.

I cradled her inside of my arms and she and I talked to one another all night long until we fell asleep. Waking up out of my sleep to check my surroundings was something that I did whenever I fell asleep in unfamiliar places. I couldn't believe that I'd fell asleep next to Courtney, so instead of checking my phone like I usually did on the wake up, I admired her beauty. I caressed my hands down the side of her face and ran my hand down her neckline until I stopped in the center of her chest. She was beautiful to me while she slept, so I did what any nigga in his right mind would do if he got the chance to wake up next to her. I stole a kiss from her and pulled her closer into my chest, so that I could wrap my arm around her some more. She stirred in her sleep, so I loosened my grip on her and turned around to check my phone. It was six in the morning and my ex, Teamber had done called my phone two times and left me a voicemail. I checked on Courtney and then I got ready to get up out of her bed when I noticed someone sitting right in front of her bed with a gun pointed towards us.

"WHAT DA FUCK?" I asked Slade. "Nigga, what the fuck is you doing here? How long you been in here?"

"OH MY GOD! SLADE! WHAT? WHAT ARE YOU DOING HERE? WHAT'S GOING ON?" I turned around and stared at her before I gave my full attention back to Slade.

"The question is, what the fuck y'all got going on?" He ignored me and walked in Courtney's direction, but that ain't do shit except for piss me the fuck off.

This nigga knew who the fuck I was in the city, so for him to ignore me like he ain't know my capabilities was real disrespectful. I remained calm cause she wasn't my bitch and I wanted to see if he was gon do some shit to her to make me catch a body up in this bitch. This fuck nigga snatched back the covers and stared at Courtney.

"Slade! No! Don't!" she screamed.

"This nigga ain' gon do nothin." I reassured Courtney.

"Hmph! What y'all were in here doing? Spooning? Cuddling? So, you goin after my leftovers now, huh?"

"That ain't none of yo business. You need to go!" Courtney said to him.

Slade snatched her up by her shirt and held her up in

the air as he screamed in her face and dropped her to the floor. She balled up and from her reaction towards the shit, I could only imagine what went on in their relationship. *Ah, hell naw*, I thought to myself.

I rushed over to that nigga and turned him around, so that he was looking at me. "The fuck you think you doin?" I punched him dead in his shit and Slade and I were fighting like cats and dogs before I knew it.

I had to stop myself from shooting the nigga with his own pistol. I grabbed my tool from the nightstand inside of her room and snatched up my phone, so I could get the fuck up out of her apartment. My nerves were rattled, and I was pissed off cause I was fighting over her and I hadn't even gotten the pussy yet.

"She got me out here goin' bad," I said as I snatched my car door open.

13

Daisha

I could never get used to staying in this house with Khari or Slade. This shit was too big for it to just be the two of them living here. This nigga Slade had left me alone in his bedroom while he did God knows what. I tried to wait up on him to walk back through his bedroom door, but it was early in the morning and I had to get home, so that I could get ready for work. Something was telling me that Slade had left me alone in his room without telling me where he'd went to be messy and petty with me. I felt like he just wanted Khari to catch me leaving out of his room. He was tryna ruin my relationship even though he didn't wanna be with me.

"Selfish ass nigga," I mumbled under my breath as I got up from his bed to go inside of his bathroom.

I searched through his cabinets and found a wash towel and an oversized dry off towel to use while I was in the shower. I used the mouthwash that was sitting on his bathroom sink to rinse my mouth out, and then I dressed myself in the same outfit that I'd wore over to their house last night. My head was spinning from the lean that I'd drank last night, so I held my head down as I did my walk of shame out of their house. I heard someone cough from behind me once I got to the door. I turned around out of instinct to see who it was behind me and it was my boyfriend, Khari Perez.

"It's over. You's a bum ass, sheisty, ole dirty ass bitch. I can't believe that I was tryna fall in love with you. So, that's what your slut ass do? You go and fuck with my brother to get back at me?"

"Khari! Are you fuckin crazy? Do you hear yourself? How you gonna try and check me? How you gon ask me something like that when you just got caught fuckin another bitch last night? You made me cry! And had the nerve to lock me out yo room, like I was a fucking nobody! Had me waiting to get dressed to go out on a date witchu. Nigga, what?" I jerked my head back and looked at him like I was confused.

"It's the principle. You a woman. You can't do the shit that I can do," he had the nerve to say to me.

"Oh! It's a double standard? Huh?" I asked him before I rolled my tongue across my bottom row of teeth and looked at him with tears in my eyes.

I was only heartbroken and hurt because I knew that it

was really over between the two of us. Khari was going places in life if he didn't get involved with his family business and he could be a good man to a woman one day if he learned how to stop running away from his problems. I shifted my weight to one leg, placed my hand on my hip, and shook my damn head at him.

"I caught you and you trippin bout me fuckin another nigga."

"Yeah hoe, cause that nigga's my brotha. You know what? Get out! NOW!" he screamed. I watched the veins pop out of his neck and his skin turn red.

It didn't feel good when I dished the same shit out to him, but Khari wasn't a weak nigga. He wasn't going for none of my shit. Secretly, my heart was crushing inside of my chest because I wanted him. I wanted to be with him because I didn't have much going for myself and I needed a man like him to raise some children with. He walked towards me with his fists balled up like he was ready to bust a move or something, so I waited on it because I knew that he knew better than to put his motherfuckin hands on me.

"I ain't never hit a woman before, but you make me wanna beat yo ass," he said to me.

"You bad." I challenged him.

Khari glared at me and stepped around me to open the door, so that I could leave. There was nothing else that I could say to him because I knew how he felt about me cheating and creeping on him. He was the jealous type and he meant what he said when he told me that I couldn't be on the shit that he was on when it came to me giving up the pussy to another nigga. I walked out of the house, trying to keep my pride and dignity. I held back my tears until I got to the driver's door of my car. I wanted to turn around and look back at him because he was going off to college soon and I might not ever see him again. The love that was shared between me and Khari was real, yet love wasn't going to repair the damage that I'd done to our relationship. I opened the driver's door of my car, sat down inside of the driver's seat, and broke down into tears as I pulled my seatbelt across my chest.

"What did I just do? I asked myself. "I lost him! I lost him!" I cried out as I started the engine of my car.

I drove home, regretting the fact that I ever fucked with his brother, but he made me feel something that Khari didn't make me feel. Slade made me feel like he loved me and my pussy. Plus, I'd promised him that this pussy was his, so I started to wonder as I drove to my mama's house. The nigga didn't strap up when he was fucking me, yet he didn't nut inside of me either. He lost his shit when he found out that his homeboy had nutted inside of his bitch. It was my duty to make him forget all about her, Miss Courtney. My heart was broken, but I couldn't stop weighing my options.

"Should I fight for my relationship with Khari or should I fuck his brother's head up and get with him?" I asked myself. *"He loves me,"* I kept telling myself since Slade fucked me without using protection.

I knew where he was going to be, so I got dressed as soon as I got inside of the house. I had on a short ass spaghetti strapped beige dress to catch his attention since I knew that nine times out of ten Slade was going to be on the block. My thoughts were on catching his eye and holding his attention cause all I ever dreamt about was bagging a rich ass nigga.

"He gon be mad jealous when another nigga try to holla at me," I laughed as I walked out the door with my phone in my hand.

I was texting some of my other friends to tell them to meet me on the stoop, so I wouldn't have to sit by myself and look like a bird out here this early in the morning. Me, Resha, and Jalissa posted up against the brick walls of the project houses and watched the boys in the hood trap and dap each other up while they talked big shit. We went back and forth from the basketball courts to the sidewalk. The only thing that we could do in the hood was have water balloon fights, watch the niggas, and walk up and down the blocks to try to be one of the chosen ones that caught a nigga's attention. It was hot as fuck outside, so me and my girls stopped walking up and down the sidewalk to post up and watch the niggas that were some big hustlers. We stood there looking and gossiping until Slade and I locked eyes with each other. I looked down at my phone in my hand and pursed my lips at him cause we didn't exchange phone numbers or nothing, so I got in my feelings. I felt sad inside, but I knew what to do. I was going to give him something to see, then maybe he'd change his mind about me. I talked to a few of them lame ass niggas to piss him off and get a reaction out of him. It worked too cause Slade walked over to where I stood talking to one of them niggas and broke that shit up.

"Boy bye!" I snapped and rolled my eyes at him.

He gripped me by my neck and kissed me in front of all them people. I got mad at him because I was used to being discreet with my personal affairs. My relationships were always private because I didn't like for people to be in my business at all.

"I'll take you down right here, right now," he said to me.

I used my tongue to lick his bottom lip before I kissed him again.

"Mmm, right now?" I moaned in between his lips.

"Follow me home," he released his grip on my neck

and looked around at the people that were staring and talking about us.

"Okay," I nervously said to him before he kissed me again.

"Don't play," he told me before he took a few steps back from me.

"These people gon be talkin. Stop Slade!" I giggled.

"They gon hate you anyway. Give me the pussy," he said through a devilish grin.

"I'm on the way. I'm coming," I told him.

The whole hood was watching us, but we didn't give a damn, so I waved bye to my friends and walked in the direction of my car while Slade dapped up his friends and told them bye. I sat in my car, waiting for him, and then I pulled off behind him. I followed him home and prayed to God that Khari was still gone.

"Damn, we bout to do this shit again," I said aloud to myself in my car as I felt the butterflies flutter inside of my stomach.

I got out of my car and followed Slade up to his doorway. He pushed open the door and allowed me to walk inside of his house before him. I stood there near the bottom of his staircase and turned around to look back at him.

"You know where my room is," he said to me as he locked the deadbolt of his house door.

I walked up the stairs to his bedroom and sat down on his bed with my clothes on.

"You ready?" I watched Slade come up out of his shirt and instantly got wet just by looking at him.

"Mmhhhmm!" I moaned as I wiggled on the bed like a kid receiving a present.

"Get naked then," he commanded me.

I started to undress myself and then I laid back on his

bed. He climbed on top of me and stared at me before he rubbed his hands against my pussy lips. I closed my eyes and kept them shut tightly as I breathed heavily in anticipation of him entering inside of me.

"Ugh!" I gasped as he inserted his index and middle finger inside of me. I clasped my hands against my lips and waited for him.

"Let me see how wet that pussy get for me." Slade twirled his fingers inside of my pussy and made me squirm and grind on his fingers.

I opened my eyes and fucked his fingers while I licked my lips and stared at him.

"You gon make me. Come here girl," he said as he plunged his fingers inside of my mouth and pulled me downward towards him.

Slade lifted my legs over his shoulder and tapped the head of his dick against my pussy two to three times before he shoved his dick inside of me.

"YES!" I screamed out in pain and pleasure.

"You want some more of this dick?"

"Yes! I want it! I want it!" I wrapped my arms around his neck and tried my best to take all of him.

14

Khari

I was up all night last night feeling guilty cause I got caught cheating on my bitch with some random ass hoe. I contemplated calling Daisha to apologize to her for what she'd saw. It hurt me that I'd hurt her, yet I wasn't tryna face the music and hear her curse me out like I was a dog. I knew it was wrong that I shut my room door in her face and ran from the issue that was standing in between us. I just couldn't keep my dick in my pants when it came to being faithful in my relationships. I thought that I'd be able to be faithful with Daisha because my girl looked good, was crazy, and a fun girlfriend to have, but I still cheated on her ass. My heart couldn't accept the fact that I'd done that to Daisha because I wasn't that type of nigga that would do anything to hurt her, at least not intentionally.

I'd told myself this morning when I woke up that I was going to go see her and apologize with some roses, a card, or some romantic ass shit. My words were going to mean nothing to her, so I was going to have to show Daisha that I was serious about being with her. I knew that I was going to have to promise her that I'd never cheat on her again or take her love for granted and I meant it. I would never fuck around on her again and I'd remain faithful to her this time around, but first she'd have to forgive me.

I kept calling her phone all morning long, but got no response from her, not even a text back. I was up all morning beating myself up about my stupid ass decision. I tried to call her again before I got ready to meet my home-boys to practice and condition our footwork with the ball, but I was getting the voicemail now. My heart was torn, so I said that I was going to go straight to her mama's house to see her first. I was on my way to the house door when I noticed her figure on the staircase inside of my house that I shared with my brother, Paiton. I snapped on her ass cause she was on some crucial get back shit.

I was ready to kill my bitch over the fuck shit that she'd done to get back at a nigga. You don't get a nigga back like that, but Daisha was different cause she moved like a nigga. I called Mya after I read Daisha and gave her a piece of my mind, but Mya didn't answer the phone for me. I sat inside of my car, contemplating where I was about to go, and what I should do to numb the pain that was in my chest from my girl fucking my brother to get back at me. I drove to the park to chill with my friends, but they wouldn't understand the shit that was going through my head. I tried to tell them what was going on and explain to them the lifestyle that I lived, but they didn't feel me, so I left the park and drove to the hood. I contemplated smoking some weed or buying up some edibles to get high for the day just so I wouldn't have to feel a damn thing.

I loved my bitch, but neither one of us knew how to be in a committed relationship with each other. I was chilling in the hood, but everybody was looking at me funny like I didn't belong over there, so I made my purchase of some edibles and three grams of weed from the pushers that worked for my brother. Them niggas was acting real weird, so I got my shit, and sat inside of my car thinking bout Daisha and rolling up a blunt. I tried to occupy my time, but I ended up looking at pictures of her. I started up my car and drove to the house, so I could smoke the loud pack of gas that I'd just bought. I pulled up at the house and squinted my eyes as I cursed inside of my head. I knew damn well that Daisha had left before me, but her car was now in the driveway parked behind my brother's shit.

"Damn, she still fuckin my bro?" I shook my head knowing the answer to my own question and got out of my car. "That bitch ain't never love me," I said aloud as I tried my best to unlock the front door of the house.

I couldn't get inside of the house because the deadbolt was locked, so I walked around the back of the house to try the back door. I walked inside of the house irritated because Slade and I never locked the top lock on the front door. My mind was blown as I listened to the moans coming from upstairs. I walked to the front door to unlock the deadbolt on the house door and walked out of the house. I made sure that I slammed the door behind me in hopes that it would get their attention. I lit up the blunt and drove over to Courtney's house to tell her the shit that my brother was doing. I felt like he never deserved her from the beginning anyway because she was always trying to be damn near perfect for him. I sprayed some blunt spray inside of my car and then I rushed up to her front door to knock like something was wrong. She came to the door with a look of concern on her face.

"Khari? What's up?" She asked me.

"I won't stay long." I told her before she took a few steps back to let me inside of her apartment.

I rushed in to hug her because I couldn't help it. I couldn't help myself, so I placed my head on her shoulder and cried. She pried my hands from around her waist to looked me in my face.

"What's going on? What's wrong?" she asked me.

I told Courtney what the fuck was going on between my girl and my brother. Daisha wasn't my bitch no more, but I still had feelings for the hoe. She was my first love, my everything, and the first girl to ever break my heart. I watched her keep her composure and show no emotion as I told her about the two of them together and how they were fucking every chance that they could get. Courtney did the lame shit that she always did when it came to Paiton "Slade" Hernandez; she took up for him and said nice things to make him seem like he was more than what he was. Everybody knew that nigga wasn't shit. He didn't care about nothing or nobody. I loved the fact that Courtney always said encouraging words to me and made me feel like I was more than just some dope boy or a nigga that had to hustle to get my money and make ends meet. She was always so positive and upbeat about everything regardless of what that nigga was taking her through.

"Who is he?" AD came out of her room and asked her.

"UGH! Adric, this is Khari. He's um. Slade's baby brother," she told him.

"What's up? You know me," I told him as I extended my hand out to shake his hand like we were people.

He shook my hand and looked at Courtney like he was telling her to get rid of me.

"Yeah, what's up. What you want?" he asked me.

"He came to tell me that his brother is seeing someone else," Courtney started, but he held up his hand to stop her.

"I wasn't talking to you. I was talking to him," Adric told Courtney.

She jerked her head back and raised her eyebrow at him.

"Yeah, that's what I was telling her," I told him. "I'll holla at you later Courtney," I said as I leaned in for a hug and turned around, so she could walk me out of her apartment.

"You sure you okay?" she asked me.

Niggas couldn't help, but to love Courtney cause she made every nigga from the hood feel like they were some-body. My brother kept her on a tight leash and kept her to himself, but she was always sweet to everyone that she met. I smiled at her and nodded my head.

"I'm okay. Stay up in life," I told her before I opened her apartment door to walk out.

I thought about how I was going to get my brother back for the shit that he was doing and drove over to the trap. I knew that the only way to fuck with him was to fuck with his money, so I thought about learning the dope game and going all in. I was walking towards the bando where my brother's workers cooked up and bagged the weed, pills, and shit. A fine, thick bitch was strolling up the block, so I stopped her to get her name just in case I saw her again. I couldn't stop looking at the curves on her body and thinking about all the things that I wanted to do to her. My heart wanted to move on from Daisha and the bullshit that she'd did to me, so I asked the girl for her phone number. I was surprised that she gave it to me without me having to ask her more than twice for it. She told me that her name was Britin, and I was looking forward to getting to know her on a more personal level, but right now I was more interested in handling my business.

"I ain' never seen you around here," she commented while I saved her name and number in my contacts list.

"Yeah, I don't usually come over here like that, but you gon see me around more often. Look, I've gotta get going, but I'mma hit you up later though," I told her.

"Alright. Call me." Britin winked her eye and licked her lips at me.

"Oh, she a freak," I said to myself.

I winked my eye back at her and wished that I had the time to fuck around with her, but I wasn't interested in fucking. I'd rather get me some money, plus my brother's betrayal had turned my heart cold. I walked in the direction of the trap spot, knocked on the door, and waited for them niggas to let me inside.

"Yyyoooo! What you doin here?" one of Slade's workers asked me.

"I came to learn. I'm tryna get down wit y'all," I told him.

"You sure you ready for this life? What yo pops say?" Kyree asked me.

"Yeah, I'm ready. I ain' gotta ask my pops for permission to do shit. Shit, he been waiting for me to jump headfirst in this shit. All he ever wanted was for me to trap and get money wit him." I pushed the nigga out my way and walked inside of the trap spot like I owned that bitch.

"Sssshhhiiiddd! I can't stop you if this what you wanna do young nigga," Kyree said as he followed behind me inside of the bando. "Young Perez said he wanna get down wit us. Show em around," he told the other nigga that were cookin up dope inside of the kitchen.

I chilled with them niggas and learned as much as the game as I could from them within the few hours that I was there in the trap house with them. I text that bitch Britin while I was there and made plans to get up with her until my brother came through to check on his operation. We stared at each other eye to eye when he walked inside of his trap house.

"Baby bruh!" he said as he walked over to the table where I sat bagging up cocaine, weed, and pills.

"You done fucking my old bitch now?" I asked him.

"You can't let that shit interfere with getting this money nigga. Bros before hoes. You know the motherfuckin motto my nigga," he told me.

"Yeah, you right." I agreed with him because blood was thicker than water and Slade was still gonna be my brother at the end of the day.

I wasn't tripping over Daisha; it was the principle of him disrespecting the bro code when it came down to my lady. Revenge was going to be sweet whether he knew it or not, but I knew how I had to play this shit to get back at him. I kept quiet and watched how they operated, so I'd know how to slang dope and make a name for myself.

15

Britin

I was in my feelings all morning because I'd been up calling Slade's phone all night and he wasn't answering. I hated when he made me feel like I was an option and acted like there wasn't other niggas out here that wanted to be with me. I mean, I wasn't going to be available or dumb for him like my friend Courtney was for him. That's all a nigga wanted was for a bitch to play stupid and I wasn't with that shit cause I could get any nigga that I wanted. I had to remind myself who the fuck I was this morning cause if I didn't, then I would've been depressed and in the bed, eating ice cream all damn day.

I got up, got dressed, and did my make-up cause it wasn't like Slade to not pop up on the block. I walked outside to these hoes looking at me like they had some tea to spill. It was a beautiful day outside today, so I walked over to the clique of girls that I normally rolled with whenever Courtney wasn't in the hood chilling with me and sat down on the stoop beside them.

"Y'all seen Slade come through here today?"

"Gggiirrrllll!" They all chimed in behind each other.

"What?" I asked them, ready for the tea.

I listened to them hoes tell me everything that they'd seen happen between Slade and Daisha. I had a hard time hiding my anger and jealousy because the nigga had me feeling like we were supposed to be together. I'd loved him way before my girl was his girlfriend, but niggas always overlooked bitches like me. They swore that we were taken or full of ourselves, but all we really wanted was a real love.

I had to pretend like I didn't care because none of these bitches knew that I was fuckin Slade behind Courtney's back. I promised myself that I was through with him since he wanted to repay me like this after I'd just told him how I felt about him again. It was like the nigga got off on knowing that I was going to keep believing every lie that he fed me, but I wasn't Courtney. I wasn't a dumb broad that wanted him for the glitz, glamor, and the money that he had surrounding him.

"I can't go tellin Courtney no shit that y'all think y'all seen. Tell me again," I said to them.

I listened attentively to make sure that I'd heard them correctly when they told me that Slade was kissing a bitch in front of the whole hood like him and Courtney wasn't known for going back to each other. I smirked and put on a happy face like everything was okay since he wasn't my man anyway. That shit was killing me inside cause I didn't know shit about Slade being with another hoe, but then again somebody had answered his phone when I called him this morning. I thought that it was Slade answering the phone in his sleep, but it must've been that new bitch that he was fucking with. I looked away from them and saw his brother getting out of his big boy truck and walking towards us.

"Oh, there go his brother. Lemme ask him who the fuck this bitch is." I stood up and walked down the steps to walk towards Khari.

I couldn't ask him right off the bat if he knew who his brother was fuckin round with, so I made small talk with him and made him think that I was interested in him. I knew that my body would catch his eye and grab his attention. He'd be too busy looking at my curves and my figure to realize a damn thing that I was saying to him. Most men fell for my bullshit and gave in to me with the quickness, so this wasn't going to be a challenge for me at all. I told him that I'd never seen him come through to the hood before and Khari told me that I'd be seeing him around here more. He asked me for my phone number, so I gave it to him and wondered if he was single or taken. I saw getting with Slade's brother as the perfect opportunity for me to get back at Slade for him playing with my feelings.

Khari was texting me within minutes, so I knew that I had that nigga exactly where I wanted him. I mentioned what my girls had told me about his brother when I responded back to his text message. He responded back to me that he'd caught his girl fuckin Slade this morning and that she was back at the house after he'd caught them together. I was sitting outside gossiping with my girls, putting two and two together, and fuming with envy.

Khari told me that he'd just left Courtney's house telling her about what he'd heard and seen when that nigga Adric came out of her bedroom. My blood started boiling because Courtney never had to fend for herself and suffer like the rest of us regular ass bitches. She didn't come from a wealthy family or have nothing, but the niggas that chose her always made sure that she was straight. It was like she basically shitted on us project bitches that were tryna come up.

I stormed off into my mama's apartment because I was so fucking jealous, and I envied her. I hated my friend so much. I'd lost Slade to a bitch that I didn't even know a damn thing about, and Courtney had already moved on and had a new man in her life. I'd heard that Adric Hernandez was a baller, so I thought of ways that I could sabotage her relationship with him. I couldn't stand to see the bitch happier than I was even if she was my best friend.

Me: Thank you Khari. Let me check on my girl and make sure she's straight.

I was on ten and mad as hell, so I wasn't trying to call Courtney and check on her. "Fuck her!" I screamed cause my issue was with her man. I called Slade's phone to see where the hell he was at and thought about pulling up on his black ass to give him a piece of my mind. This man didn't have the decency to pick up the phone when I called him, but it was okay because I knew how to get back at him for playing with my feelings like that.

I was hurt cause there wasn't going to be no more friendship between me and Courtney if she found out that I'd been sleeping with Slade behind her back. She should've been peeped the shit, but she was so naïve to shit. It made me feel bad for her, but I couldn't feel bad for a lucky ass, spoiled bitch. I got up from my bed and walked over to my closet. It was the weekend and I was finna make Paiton "Slade" Hernandez feel me. I pressed Courtney's contact ID as I opened my closet to look for me something fly to wear.

"He played me!" I yelled as I found a cute ass outfit to wear out to the club tonight. Now, all I needed to do was get Courtney's ass there, so I could fuck his head up since he wanted to play me like some lame ass bitch.

"Hey girl!" I cheered when Courtney answered the phone.

"Hey," she laughed.

"What you doing tonight?" I asked her.

"Uh! I hadn't planned on doing nothing. Why? What's up?"

"Ggggiirrrllll! I hate to be the bearer of bad news, but that nigga Slade. Girl, he got you out here looking like a damn fool. His brother told me that he done moved on from you." I said things the way that I said them in hopes that I was cutting her deep with my words.

We used to be friends, but now I wanted to see her suffer and get it on her own without the help of a man. I wondered what the fuck she was going to do now that Slade was onto a new bitch. I'd asked around about this nigga Adric and I was told that he was never seen with a bitch, ever. I turned my nose up when I heard a man's voice in the background. I figured it was him, but like I said. I'd asked around about this nigga, and the girls told me that he wasn't easy to get with. They said that he curved every single bitch that tried to get with him, but I couldn't help but to wonder why he always curved these bitches.

I listened at Courtney giggle, so I rolled my eyes in irritation because she was happy while I was here, miserable.

"Yeah, he stopped by here to tell me, but um," she

93

giggled again. "Adric's over here, and I'mma," she laughed. "I'mma call you back when he leaves. Sssttooooppp!" she laughed hard as hell.

"Hold up! I was calling you to see if you wanted to go out with me tonight?" I tried my luck at getting her out of the house, so Slade would come through to the club tonight.

This nigga was crazy in love with her. They had the weirdest relationship cause even though he damn sure didn't want her anymore, he still showed up wherever she was at. The whole hood knew how much she meant to him cause he always expressed the way that he felt about her whenever he was sloppy drunk and fucked up off them pills or something.

"Naw girl. I'm good," she said, turning me down, and making me smack my teeth in irritation.

"Come on. Do this for me. Come hang out with your best friend," I said trying to convince her to get out the house, so that I could see Slade again.

"Um. Okay, okay. Let me call you back girl cause. AD! Stop it!" she squealed. "I've gotta go girl," she laughed.

I fucking hated her guts. I pulled my freakum dress outta my closet and went back out the door to see what the block was looking like. Maybe one of them niggas that AD was chillin with the other day would be over here. I was disappointed when none of his friends were in the hood, but Khari was standing near my mama's apartment talking to that bitch, Mya. She was one of the baddest out here in the city, so I was trying to figure out why she was in Khari's face when she had a good, paid ass man that drew up blueprints for a living. She'd bagged a rich nigga that was an architect.

"What's she doing back over here?" I asked my girls.

"That bitch didn't know what she had and done left that man," my friend told me.

"Nnnnaaahhh!" I stressed.

"Mmmhhhmm!" one of the girls agreed.

I pretended as if I was walking to the trap house to buy something to eavesdrop on their conversation since I was texting Khari now.

"I'mma bag that," I told myself as I admired his muscles.

"I cheated on my nigga for you and you tellin me that you don't want me?" Mya asked Khari. "My man dumped me!" she said to him.

"Ooop!" I said as I turned around to walk back towards them to hear some more of their conversation without them noticing me.

"Well, bitch. Yeen finna get with me. I ain' no rebound ass nigga for you to come running to cause what you had wit your dude is finished," he told her.

"He broke up with me because I was with you. I turned my phone off while we were together, and he just knew. He knew that I was out cheating on him, but I couldn't tell him the truth. Khari, what am I supposed to do?"

"I don't know, but don't expect me to get witchu just cause you're single. Shit, my bitch caught us, too, so what?" he asked Mya. "I'm single, too, but I just can get wit you just cause we fucked. Ion know you like that. Plus, you disrespectful as fuck. Get back bitch." He left her standing there looking stupid.

"I've got to get him," I told myself as I walked back home to get dressed to go out to the club tonight.

16

Mya
_____

"The nerve of this nigga!" I was standing in my mama's screen door looking at the bum ass bitches and whack ass niggas that didn't have nothing better to do than stand around in the project's half the damn day.

I couldn't believe that I was back here in the slums at my mama's house living like this. I went to bed listening to her complain and woke up to her fussing about something that needed repairing inside of the small three-bedroom apartment. Damn, I couldn't wait until I could get up out of here.

I knew it was over between me and Idris and that he wasn't going to take me back since I was dishonest with him. The only thoughts that were racing through my head was my next victim and how I was gonna come up off a nigga. Shit, a bitch wasn't used to working. All I ever had to do was do a lil easy work and be cute, but my mama wasn't goin for that shit. I couldn't just lay around her house, so she made it her business to wake me up like the old folks did when the six o'clock morning news came on. I hated that shit, but I got up and cleaned her house before I got dressed and went to work every morning.

Today was different though because it was a good ass motherfuckin Friday. I was off work today, so I made plans to go out to the club with my girls. I had the best makeup, perfume, and the hottest clothes because I work at a Belk's store in the mall. Usually, I didn't get Fridays off, and I'd have to rush to get ready to go out with my friends and them, but today, I was going to be on some hot girl shit, so I could catch the eyes of all the ballers that was on the block. They were sure to be at the club tonight since it was the first of the month and them hustlers knew how and where to get their check.

A bitch like me was gonna be sitting in the cut, scoping out the nigga that the money was coming to, and picking the right time to get up and flex this bangin body that the good Lord blessed me with. I pushed my mama's screen door open and walked right over to Khari's fine ass. I mean, he was a young nigga and everything, but the dick had me sprung.

Khari was standing there talking to Britin, and I couldn't stand the whore cause she and Rachael were the baddest two bitches out the projects. I came close to matching their assets, but I didn't have the titties to match my fat ass. Plus, I wasn't fucking a nigga for no money or tryna trap him with no damn baby. I'd rather go to college and make something out of myself and spend my own motherfucking money when and where I wanted it. I'd just lost my nigga over fucking with this nigga but seeing him smile in front of Britin made me so jealous. I wanted to be the reason for his smiles and shit. I was on ten tryna break that shit up cause I'd just checked this hoe about being up in my niggas' faces and here she was tryna fuck with the nigga that had just made me cum less than twenty-four hours ago.

"Ole sneaky ass hoe!" I fussed as I rolled my eyes at every bitch that looked my way.

A hoe didn't have shit on me cause I could take their nigga on a bad day. It was true; I was a little stuck up and bourgeoise, but I had every reason to be cause I was nothing like them other bitches. Britin walked off just in time cause she must've forgot what I done to her the last time that I saw her ass. Khari walked in the opposite direction to his brother's trap spot, but I knew I couldn't go inside of there cause then my mama would've been talking bout kicking me out. She always swore that I was on some shit whenever I wasn't swimming in money or finessing the fuck out of a nigga. All she really cared about was having money to spend, so that she could live outside of her means.

I must say that I'd inherited that greed trait from her cause now I was blowing money that I knew my ass didn't have trying to keep up with these local bitches. I sucked my teeth and rolled my eyes at how this nigga has walked away from me like he didn't see me coming his way. My ego was bruised like fuck cause I knew that my sex game was stupid, and he wasn't even sweating me like

I thought he would after I'd fucked him silly the other night.

My heart was hurting because I'd lost the man that I'd loved and the pain killer that I'd tried to take as a remedy wasn't doing nothing for me. Khari was the pain killer and I thought that our one night together would turn into me taking another dose of him every time that I felt lonely or needed another dose of him. I walked over to the bitches that were beneath me and listened to the gossip of how Slade had come over here and pretty much showed everybody who his new bitch was going to be.

"Daisha?" I snapped my head back like I was saying, "Come again," and then I tuned up my nose and lips. "Ain't that his brother girl?" I asked to be messy and put it out there in the open. "I'll holla at y'all later. Y'all coming to the club tonight, right?" I asked the girls.

"We gon be in there!" they chimed in.

"Aight then. Let me go holla at this nigga real quick," I told them before I walked off to go and give Khari a piece of my mind.

This nigga was out here acting like I wasn't nobody. Ugh uhn, I wasn't having that cause I'd never had a nigga not come back and fuck with me, so he was mistaken or either I didn't put it on him good enough. I applied my lip gloss on my lips and sexily walked over to him to remind him why he cheated on his girlfriend with me in the first place. We stood there fussing and going back and forth with each other about what the fuck he thought he should be doing, but he just wasn't getting it.

Khari was standing here acting like he was a heartless ass nigga, but he didn't know that the more that he tried to deny his attraction for me, the more that I was going to fuckin remind him why I was that bitch. See, a nigga like Khari was every woman's fantasy cause he was smart and he was going to make something out of himself. A nigga had a bitch playing her cards right cause any other hoe in her right mind would've punctured the condom or told his bitch about us fucking each other. Hell, she'd caught us together anyway, so now his ex was with his brother, but this nigga was still trippin like he ain' want me.

"I cheated on my nigga for you and you tellin me that you don't want me?" I asked him with my eyes full of tears.

"Well, bitch. Yeen finna get with me. I ain' no rebound ass nigga for you to come running to cause what you had wit your dude is finished," he said.

"He broke up with me because I was with you. I turned my phone off while we were together, and he just knew. He knew that I was out cheating, but I couldn't tell him the truth. Khari, what am I supposed to do?"

"I don't know, but don't expect me to get witchu just cause you're single. Shit, my bitch caught us, too, so what?" Khari looked away from me like he didn't care what I had to say to him, but then he looked me dead in my eyes to tell me how he really felt about me. "I'm single, too, but I just can get wit you just cause we fucked. Ion know you like that, plus you disrespectful as fuck. Get back bitch," he told me before he left me standing there looking like a fucking fool.

It took everything in me to keep my composure and contain myself from reaching my hands out and grabbing him by his fucking neck. I wanted to snap his neck in half for the way that he was talking to me like I was some jump off or some shit. Nah, I was that bitch and I could be the bitch for him, but he ain't want me. He'd made it perfectly clear that he didn't want to be with me, so I knew what I had to do. I had to get under somebody new to get my mind off him. They say, "To get over somebody, then you've gotta get under somebody new," and that was exactly what I was about to do. I sucked that shit up and took the loss like a gangsta as I held my head high and walked back inside of my mama's house. I went inside of my old room and turned on my old boom-box that I'd had growing up. I didn't know what CD was inside, but I heard Ciara's voice boom through the speakers. It was her Evolution CD, so I turned to one of my favorite songs by her titled, "That's Right" and sang aloud to the lyrics of the song.

I found something to wear out to the club and told myself that I had to stop looking down on these bitches and make more friends since I'm newly single. My romper fitted my body perfectly and I looked good as fuck, so I walked out of my bedroom to flex in front of the wall mirror that was up against the hallway that led to the bedrooms in my mama's apartment. I smacked my lips together and touched my stomach and ass while I checked out every angle in the mirror.

"Where the hell you think you going dressed like that?" My mama, Mildred, asked me.

"I'm bout to go out to the club and bag me a rich man," I laughed and turned away from the mirror to walk back towards my bedroom.

"What yo young ass need to be tryna do is make it work with that man, Idris."

There she was giving me unwanted advice again about what she thought was best for me. It was discouraging when people judged your life when they were on the outside looking in. That man wanted somebody to come home to, but he didn't know the first thing about loving a woman like me. I needed my independence, and I didn't want to be with a man just because he had a good job or because he had long money. There were some values that I still believed in and being with someone for what they could do for you and give you just had never been me. If you took away the sex, then what was left between two people? The vibes and the energy had to be perfect for it to work between two people and they had to communicate and trust one another.

"Ma! I don't wanna hear it."

I tried to say it in a respectful way, so that she wouldn't take offense to what I was trying to tell her.

"Don't come back to my house and think that you can talk to me like you living in your own shit or like you paying any of the bills in this bitch. This my shit! You understand me?" Mildred asked me.

I rolled my eyes. "Let me go, so I can bag me a rich nigga and get the fuck up out of yo shit. The nigga that I cheated on Idris with said that I was disrespectful as fuck anyway," I told her.

"AND HE WAS RIGHT! Get yo ass out of my house!" she yelled and swatted her hand at me.

I hated living with my mama. I stormed out of her house and got inside of my car to text a few of the bitches that I used from time to time, so that I wouldn't have to go out or walk inside of the club alone. Them bitches were ready to party, but I was more of a pre-gaming type of bitch cause I didn't have money to spend like that. I got my money's worth before I went inside of the club, but more than likely a man would buy me rounds from the bar just because my booty was poppin. Me and three other bitches bought our own bottles each and we mixed our drinks by pouring up cups and taking shots of the liquor before we went inside of the club. We were fucked up when we walked through the doors, but I didn't want to remember a damn thing about tonight unless I was leaving with Khari or a boss ass nigga.

"Mmmm! Them niggas showing out tonight!" I sang as

I led the pack and sashayed towards a sitting area in the spot.

I had to act like I was used to the shit, and like them niggas that were throwing money up in the air and showing their jewelry off was something that I was used to. My eyes scanned the room and then I saw the head huncho of the clique. It was that nigga in the city; the plug and the connect, Adric "AD" Hernandez. Shit, the nigga looked fine, fit, and good as shit. Adric had lllllooooonnnnnggggg dope money and all I could think about was fucking him on top of some money like a fuckin porn star. He saw me looking at him, so he smiled at me and continued acting like he was the owned the club or something.

"Hmph! I'mma give em somethin to look at," I said to myself as I stood up and bounced my ass up and down in a stance. "You hoes thirsty?" I looked back and asked my friends.

"Bitch, we drunk as fuck! You know we ain' got no money! Girl, I'm waiting on a nigga to throw me some bread!" each one of them hoes said.

"Baby, closed mouths don't get fed. Get the fuck up! You see these niggas in here?" I pointed at all the niggas that had that check. "You betta make that ass twerk or do something to make a nigga remember ya," I schooled them.

I rolled my eyes cause I hated when a project bitch acted simple like she ain't know how the fuck she was supposed to come up out of there. I left them standing right there and walked through the club like I was the baddest bitch up in that bitch. I stopped along the way and gave my ass a lil shake here and there. I put my hands up on my knees and rolled my hips, but I saved the best for last when I stopped right in front of him and gave him something good to see. My mama didn't have to teach me how to entice a nigga, but I wanted Adric to know that I could swirl my body on his dick just like the machine swirled ice cream on top of an ice cream cone. I put on a show for him and then a man stepped up to me. It was Jeremiah's quiet ass, so I blinked my eyes repeatedly and copped an attitude with him.

"UGH! What the fuck this nigga want?" I asked myself. "Um, when you started running with AD them?" I gave him the stank face and looked at him like he was bothering me.

"I ain' wit them. I'm my own man." He sounded like he was tryna convince me that he was a big bag having ass nigga.

Shid, I wasn't tryna go from something to nothing and I damn sure wasn't tryna help a nigga come up either. I mean, we could build together, but I wasn't raising no man or coming up off no cash to put a nigga on. I wanted to see what Jeremiah could possibly bring to the table, so I gave him some talk time, just so them other niggas could look at me.

"So, what you want?" I asked him seductively.

His eyes got big at the sound of my voice cause he ain't know that I could talk to him like that.

"You gon stop playin and give me yo phone number?"

"Nnnnooooopppeee," I giggled and placed my palms against the bar to show off my fat ass.

"Damn, you bad! So, you gon make me miss you?"

"Yeen stun me, plus I'm dealin wit a heartbreak right now," I told him.

I wasn't doing shit, but running game on him to gain his sympathy, so he'd fall for my shit and do all the things that Idris used to do for me.

"Okay miss," Jeremiah said.

I felt like he gave up too easy, so I turned up my lips, and rolled my eyes up in the air.

"Go figures!" I threw my hands up in the air cause I was expecting him to beg me for my number and buy me a drink from the bar. "Broke ass nigga," I said underneath my breath.

I looked in his direction and saw the wad of money that he had in his hand, so I sat back and chilled for ten minutes. The next thing I knew, me and my friends were walking through the crowd on the dance floor. I was headed to give Jeremiah my phone number when Adric stopped me. He told me how pretty I looked and that he'd been peeping me all night long before he asked me for my phone number. I gave both Adric and Jeremiah my phone number in the club and felt like I was that bitch cause I was bound to come up off one of them niggas.

17

Courtney

I woke up this morning with a hangover out of this world. My head was pounding, and I could barely focus, but that didn't make me forget about the sexcapade that I'd shared with Jeremiah, Slade, and Khari's girlfriend, Daisha. I tried everything to make sure that Jeremiah's sperm wouldn't fertilize an egg inside of me. I tried to drink it away, smoke it away, and if my pussy wasn't sore, then I would've fucked a random nigga last night to numb my pain.

It was difficult being loved by everybody else except for

the one motherfucker that you wanted to feel love from. I woke up sick, throwing up, and feeling dehydrated as fuck, but I knew the dangerous game that I was playing. I wanted to die so bad, but God wouldn't take me away from the life of misery that I was living.

I got up from off the floor in my bathroom and stood in front of the sink, looking at myself with disgust and feeling self-pity for myself. I didn't know that I could hate myself this much. I never imagined that I'd be doing this. That I'd be getting dressed to go to the pharmacy to pick up a Plan B prescription pill. I always wanted to be a mother, but I wasn't having a baby by a man that didn't love me and that didn't want to be with me and only me. I didn't even know this nigga, so why would I let his seed grow inside of me?

I was slipping my foot inside of a pair of Nike slide sandals when my doorbell startled me. I grabbed my wallet and my car keys to rush to the door, so that I could get rid of this baby and get over this hangover. I opened the door, but there was nobody there, so I smacked my lips and wrinkled my nose. My eyes looked down at the door mat outside of my front door, and I noticed the vase of red roses. I looked around the corner of my door to see if I could see who'd left the pretty flowers for me, but all I saw was an oversized teddy bear. I smiled and picked up the flower vase from off the door mat. I sniffed the roses and placed them on top of my kitchen bar top before I went back to the door to bring the teddy bear inside, so that I can sit him down on my couch.

"He always know how to make me smile," I said.

Slade always knew what to do to make me forgive him cause it was fucked up what he did to me. He knew better than to let me catch him with another bitch and share me with his friend. Slade had given me that lean and ecstasy pill on purpose, but I should've known better. The nigga was so fucked up in the head and was always doing shit to hurt me. I picked up my keys and my wallet off the vacant seat on my couch and tried to go to the store again. I opened my house door and there he stood, so I smiled at him and said fuck going to the store.

"Hey Slade!" I was cheesing hard as hell cause it was always the thought that counted with me.

"Where you headed?" he asked me.

"To the store to get this Plan B." I moved out his way to let him come inside of my apartment.

I closed the door behind me because he was already making himself comfortable like he always did.

"Umph! I oughta fuck you up for fuckin my people," he told me.

My happiness washed away instantly. He had that effect on me. All it took was him disapproving or disagreeing with me on something. I swear, he made me weak, but I was told that a woman was supposed to let the man be superior. I had to dim my light with Slade and be who and what he wanted me to be, but I was willing to do that because he made sure that I had clothes to wear when I didn't have anything. He took me from a bad situation and forced me to grind hard to get my own money, so that I wouldn't ever have to depend on him or ask him for anything. I appreciated him for that, but now it was like he fucking hated me for getting on my shit. I could never measure up with him, and I knew that it was because I was too much for him, and he couldn't handle that shit.

"Why he always blaming me for the shit that he start?" I asked myself.

I wouldn't have been out here doing him dirty and fucking this nigga and that nigga if he had of stopped cheating on me and having me looking like a damn fool out here in these streets. I just wanted a nigga to be all about me. It wasn't fair for us to hurt everybody else that we were dealing with by continuously running back to each other, but that's what we did. I'd made myself readily available to him because I loved him. I'd always run back to him because Slade had my heart in a major way. Yeah, sometimes he was mean to me and he'd put his hands on me every now and then, but you couldn't tell me that he didn't love me. He'd never do anything to intentionally hurt me. I just wished that we could stop playing these games with each other, but he was so unforgiving. I covered my face with my hands and cried before I looked up at him.

"So, you bought me all this stuff just to come over here and say hurtful things to me?"

"I ain't bought you shit," he said to me.

"Oh." I couldn't hide my disappointment, but suddenly the doorbell interrupted me again.

Slade looked around my apartment and started going the fuck off on me, but I ignored him like I normally did when he was talking his shit. I answered the door and sighed a sigh of relief when I noticed that it was Britin. I was so thankful and grateful for her showing up because I never knew how this nigga would react when it was just me and him.

"Girl, just ignore him. Ignore Slade. He's mad at me cause I thought that he bought me these nice gifts. He tripping and going off on me for no reason," I told my friend. "Slade! Just go!" I yelled at him. "What you come over here for anyway, huh? To make sure another nigga didn't come home with me from the club last night?" I asked him.

"I'm just gon go since y'all two in here fussin and arguin," Britin said.

"Un uhn girl. Yeen gotta go. He needs to be the one to go! You ain't gotta leave," I told her in hopes that she'd stick around a little bit longer.

I never knew which side of Slade I'd get, so I didn't want her to leave me alone with him. He was good at making me feel loved one minute and like he was being genuine, but then his personality would instantly switch. It wouldn't be until after he'd hurt me that I'd find out that he was either high or on some type of drug when he'd black out on me.

"Who the fuck gave you this shit?" he pointed at the flowers and walked in the direction of the vase that sat on top of my countertop.

"If I knew who'd bought them then I wouldn't be thankin you for it," I told him.

He picked up the vase and held it up in the air as if he was about to throw the vase at me.

"What the fuck did you just say to me? Who you think you talkin to?" Slade walked up to stand chest to chest with me.

"Nigga, I ain't scared of you. You need to leave," I said through gritted teeth.

"Oh, you tryna show out cause your lil friend over here like I won't knock you the fuck out," he said before he kicked my feet from underneath me.

I held the back of ankle, cried, and rolled around on the carpet of my living room floor.

"SLADE!" Britin screamed.

"OUCH!" I cried out in agony.

"Shut the fuck up bitch!" he yelled, but I didn't know if he was talking to me or Britin.

"Oh, let me go." Britin turned around and walked towards my front door.

I wanted to beg her not to go so bad, but I didn't want

to make him angrier than he already was. I looked up and there Adric was. I saw him talking to all them other bitches in the club last night, so it made me feel like he was over me or like he was tryna get back at me and hurt my feelings.

"I see you got the gifts I sent you," AD walked through my house door and walked straight to me.

I was sitting up on my knees, looking at him, embarrassed as fuck cause I was on my living room floor. He reached his hand down to help me stand up. I winced in pain and raised my legs up. I gave him a half smile before I remembered that Britin and Slade were still inside of my apartment with us. I was wishing that there was somewhere that I could go to run away and hide from all of the humiliation.

"That was you?" I asked AD. "Oh, thank you. I-I love them," I told him before he could answer me to confirm what I already knew.

Adric's jaws clenched together and then his facial expression changed. He turned his back to me to look at them. I walked around him to step in between him and Slade, but AD looked down at me and gave me a look that told me that I'd better move out of his way.

"Keep yo hands off my bitch nigga." Adric pressed his nose up to Slade's and my eyes widened because I just knew some shit was bout to pop off between the two of them.

I'd never heard him claim me before, so I was shocked to hear him say that.

"Oh, she yo bitch now?" Slade laughed in this man's face. "That's always gon be my bitch pussy ass nigga," he said to him.

"Naw, that's all me now. I ain't gon tell you this shit no mo. Next time I'mma just shoot ya," Adric told him.

"Um, Britin. I think you and Slade need to leave," I cleared my throat to speak.

"I'mma see you," Slade said to AD before he glared at me.

Britin just stood there like she ain't hear a damn thing that I'd just said to her about her leaving up out of my shit.

Adric walked in the direction of Britin and stopped in front of her. She was standing there like she was in awe or amazed by something. I got mad at her cause she was looking at Adric like she wanted him for herself, but this was my life that I was living, and I didn't do a damn thing to make the nigga choose me.

"You can't get this dick luh baby. I'm bout to stuff it in yo friend though. Can you leave us alone please? I'm bout to drop this dick off in her real quick." My mouth dropped to the floor, but I knew that this nigga was serious. "Don't call or come by. We finna be boo'd up for the next few days," he told Britin.

Adric walked towards my house door and opened the door for them to leave my apartment. I stood there trying to find the words to say to them... bye or something, hell anything, but I was on mute. He locked the door behind them and walked over to scoop me up in his arms. He looked me deep in my eyes as he carried me to my room. AD placed me down on my back, pinned my hands down, and used his teeth to undress me. He placed soft kisses along my skin and caressed my skin before he flipped me over on my stomach.

"Tell me how much you liked your gifts," he commanded me as he smacked me hard on my ass cheeks.

"ADRIC!" I screamed.

"Girl, I ain' playin witchu. Tell me," he smacked me harder this time, so I told him what he wanted to hear.

"I loved my gifts!" I moaned and bit down on my

bottom lip.

He punished me by teasing my body with his tongue, spanking me, and pulling on my hair, so that I faced him as he bit down on my ass cheeks.

"You make me crazy," he confessed to me.

"Mmmm!" I said before I heard a condom wrapper rip open. "Uuuhh!" I gasped when he entered inside of me.

"I'mma be crazy bout you. Please, don't give this shit to no one else," he whispered in my ear while he was hitting it from the back.

"I won't," I mumbled.

"Say it louder. You betta say that shit like you fuckin mean it." Adric's voice was demanding and he spoke with authority, so it made me feel uncomfortable.

I was so used to being in control of everything and every situation, but things were different when I was with him. He placed his hands inside of mines and rolled our bodies sideways. Adric lifted one of my legs up in the air and held it up in place with his hands on the back of my thigh. He gripped my thigh tighter each time that he pulled his dick out of my pussy. He teased my entry hole with the head of his dick and made me beg him to give it to me.

"I want it Adric! Give it back! Ugh!" I reached my hand behind me to insert his dick back inside of me, but he slapped it away and pulled my head back, so that I was staring him in his face,

"You'n run shit!" he told me before he kissed me and plunged his dick deep inside of me. I gasped for air because I wasn't ready. "Now, what was that shit you was saying?" he asked me.

I rolled my eyes at him and he changed positions on me. We were now in the missionary position. I didn't want to look at him or look him in his face because he was getting the best of me. He intertwined his fingers inside of my fingers and stared into my face.

"Ion hear you." I could tell that he was fucking with me, so I played along with him.

"I want it. I fucking want it," I told him

"Mmmhuh!" he moaned and gave me the dick. "Wrap your legs around me," he instructed.

I closed my eyes and came over and over again.

"You gon let me ride it?" I asked him when I felt him tense up on me.

"Hell yeah," AD said.

I did a split on his dick, placed the palm of my hands in the center of the bed, and bounced my ass up and down before I bent forward to press my knees together and give him slow strokes and back shots of my ass going up and down on his dick. We spent the entire evening fucking until we fell asleep together.

Adric wasn't in my bed beside me when I woke up in the morning, so I felt my heart break inside my chest cause I was in love with him. I was hurt like hell because I didn't expect for him to dip out on me like that. I called my girl Britin, but I didn't tell her that me and Adric spent the day fucking, but it was already obvious. She came over to my crib and we sat on social media trying to pinpoint his whereabouts, so that I could pull up on this nigga. I don't know who he thought I was, but I wasn't some one-night stand kind of woman. I couldn't stop thinking about who else he was fucking, but it didn't take me long to find out where this nigga had gone when he left my apartment.

Britin and I pulled up to the projects to find him smiling in the face of some other woman. She was pretty as fuck, too, but she wasn't from around here. I knew all the hoes that were from the hood and this bitch wasn't one of them. I walked up on them with all the shit.

"Who is this Adric?" I used his government name to let him know that I was pissed off with him. "Who is she to you, huh?" I looked at her with an attitude and waited for her to get slick with me.

The bitch laughed at me and looked to him like he was supposed to check me about questioning who she was to him.

"Hmph!" she folded her arms across her chest and stood there beside him.

My eyes were welling up with tears at this point because we'd just made love, but he was smiling big for her.

"Leave," he said to me.

I glared at him with hate growing in my heart for him. How could he leave me like that this morning, just to go and be with some other bitch? Any other hoe would've tripped about it, but he was expecting for me to snap on him and act a fool in public. I wasn't gon give him or this woman the satisfaction of knowing how I felt about him. Ain't no telling what he was telling her when I wasn't with him, and I didn't know their situation, so who was I to judge them?

I turned around and walked away gracefully because I knew how to make him feel me. I blocked that nigga from calling my phone and on all my social media accounts cause I was going to teach him a lesson. He couldn't have me when he wanted me and he damn sure wasn't finna stop me from entertaining these other niggas that were tryna get at me. I knew better than to fuck with him. I mean, who was I kidding? He was Adric Hernandez, the connect in the city, and a fuckin ladies' man. I should've known better. I should've known that he wasn't the type to settle down and commit to one woman.

18

Adric

I got up early this morning and left Courtney's house because a nigga found himself falling for her. I had a situation going on that I'd yet to tell her about. She'd been going through her own shit, so I didn't want to disappoint her by telling her that I was involved with someone else. My heart knew who and what it wanted, but I was trying to make the best moves that would place me in a better position.

I was in the bed, admiring her facial features, and

reminiscing on the way that she'd put it down on me last night. I was feeling like I'd fell in love with shorty on sight. The shit was crazy, but it was true. It was something that I'd never want to admit to her because I didn't want her to think that she had me like that. I tried to fight what I felt for her, but I thought about having a future with her every time that I saw the girl.

I'd finally found out what she was hiding from me and why she wasn't as interested in me as she should've been when I first tried to get at her. I just wanted her to care. I wanted her to realize that I was looking for something real to come home to and someone to fucking care about me. Now, I was laying up with her with my heart torn between who I wanted to be wit and the bitch that I was playing house with on the other side of town, Teamber Singleton.

Shit, it was a pretty day outside today, so I was glad that I'd gotten my ass up out the bed to hit the hood. I had to do my thing in these streets to keep my mind off Courtney and Teamber cause I was out here pissing Teamber off by going out bad behind Courtney's inconsiderate and ungrateful ass. I hadn't never spent money or time on a female the way that I was doing with Courtney, so I told myself that I had to fall back from her.

Teamber came through the hood to see me like clockwork, so today was no different. We stood there chopping it up, laughing, and talking while I collected my money. I looked up and squinted before I placed my right hand over my eyes to block the sun. It looked like Courtney was headed my way with her friend that was over her house when I stopped by yesterday. Courtney stopped in front of me and I could see the hate in her eyes.

"Damn," I cursed myself in my head.

I thought that she was about to knock the shit out of me or act up in front of all these people, but she didn't.

Courtney was a liability because I'd heard about the way that she used to get into it with these women behind Paiton. I didn't need that in my life, and I felt like she didn't give a fuck about me, so I told myself that I had to do something to make her care for real.

"Who is this Adric?" I'd never heard her call me by my first name, so it surprised me to hear her say it. "Who is she to you, huh?" Courtney asked me.

All eyes were on me at this point cause I knew Teamber would tell Courtney some shit that would crush her fucking soul.

"Hmph!" Teamber said.

"Aww shit!" I said in my head cause Teamber would ride for a nigga.

My bitches were some fighters, but I wasn't with that fighting shit, not over no dick. Hell, they could both get this tip, but I wasn't trying to be a playa no mo. I stood there thinking of how to diffuse the situation quickly.

"Leave," was all that I could force myself to say to her.

I could see it in her eyes that she was about to cry, and I hated to be the one that caused tears to fall from her eyes. It was never my intentions to hurt her or make her feel like anything I told her wasn't true cause I was in love with her too. I'm a d-boy and I don't need Courtney rolling up on me asking me questions like she my bitch when I could've been handling my business. It was taking everything in me not to say anything spiteful or say nothing to her that would hurt her feelings. Courtney had the power to change my mood. Yeah, she had me like that; I was confused as fuck. I knew that these women could really hurt a nigga, especially if the nigga was to put all his trust in a bitch and start to fucking give a fuck. I kept telling myself that I knew her type. I told myself that she was just gon go out and fuck another nigga, but I didn't want her to do that. I wanted to make her to fall in love with me and see nobody else, but me. Yet and still, my heart was torn between the two women.

I only came to the hood today to collect my money and check on my operation, but Teamber always did the most to get my attention and keep it. I can't even lie to you, she had a piece of my heart, but I was ready to cut her off and be through with her for good. Teamber and I had a vibe and a mental connection, but I felt a forever thing whenever I was with Courtney. It was like the girl and I had soul ties. Teamber and I met six years ago, and we've been talking to each other over the years, keeping in contact, and we finally gave this relationship thing a try. It was cool and all until I realized that I couldn't stop fucking with these other hoes, so now she just plays her role. Teamber turned around and gave me that look that said, *"I thought so,"* when Courtney walked away from us.

I couldn't stand for a female to think that she had me like that, so I glared at Teamber cause she knew that I had love for her and that I wouldn't put our business out in the streets like that. I turned my back to her and started dapping up my people, so I could get the hell on. I tried to give her a hug, but she knew that a nigga was on some bull shit, so she moved her shoulder to brush me off.

"Where you going AD?" she asked me.

"I gotta go take care of something. I'm gon come through and fuck witchu later, aight?"

"Nah, you can stay wherever you at. I asked you where you going." Man, I could sense the attitude coming up off shawty, but I felt bad for how I'd just dissed my lil shawty in front of my boys, so I had to go and check on her.

I wasn't a weak ass nigga, but I wasn't to be played with either. I was mad as fuck because I had a bitch that was all about me that I didn't really want to be with and one that just didn't give a fuck about shit except for being cute and shit. A nigga was in a fucked-up predicament either way, but Courtney was giving me something that Teamber just wasn't giving me. Courtney gave my life, a reason, and a purpose. Plus, I felt like I didn't have to tell her nothing when I was around her. She understood me for who I was, and our souls were kind of like one. I felt complete when I was with her, like I ain't need nothing or no one, but her. I sprinted to my car, got inside, and started up my engine to go and check Courtney for the bullshit that she was doing. Bitch had the game all wrong, like I was her ex or somethin, but I was going to show her that I was different. I parked my car outside of her apartment complex and ran up to her door.

"Boom! Boom! Boom!" My fists pounded up against the door. "Her friend betta not be up in here with her," I said to aloud as I waited for her to come and answer the door.

"Who is it?"

"Open the door Courtney!" was all I could get out before I heard the lock turning on the door. *"Shit!"* I thought when I saw her with her sundress on.

"What do you want Adric? Why are you here?" Courtney asked me.

I stared in her face and could tell that she'd been crying.

"What you crying for? You missed me?" I laughed before I picked her up and closed her front door with the back of the heel of my shoe.

"Put me down!" she fussed, but I ignored her and fidgeted with the lock on her door until I turned the lock.

"Who you wearing that shit for?" I asked her, but she bit down on my shoulder.

"PUT. Me. Down!" she squealed as she pounded her fists against my shoulder blades and the top of my back.

I wanted her ass to myself so bad that I closed her bedroom door behind us like someone else was in her apartment with us. I gently placed her on her bed and pushed up the sundress that she was wearing. I loved the fact that she ain't have no panties on underneath it, so I rubbed my hands on the inside of her thighs and lowered my body onto the floor.

"Why you ain't got no panties on?" I breathed against her pussy and waited for her to answer me, but I knew that she was anticipating feeling my tongue touch her lips or the inside of her labia.

I licked her clit like a cat using its tongue to drink milk out of a bowl, then I placed my finger inside of her vaginal opening, so that I could pry my tongue inside of her vaginal hole. I swallowed her secretion and got excited when I heard her gasp and moan. I pulled my tongue out of her pussy to lick around her pussy before I looked up at her.

"Adric," she said my name in a low voice and looked at me with admiration in her eyes.

"You like this shit?" I asked her.

"Hmm?" she asked me, but I knew like fuck she heard me. "I love this shit," Courtney confessed to me.

I gave her more head and then I climbed on top of her to intertwine my hands inside of hers and look her inside her eyes while I fucked her slow.

"I'm sorry. I'm sorry for earlier," I told her over and over again.

"It's okay. Just don't stop. Keep going. Make love to me Adric," she said in between her moans. I felt her roll her hips underneath me and meet my strokes as I was going deep.

"Aaahh!" I moaned out in ecstasy as she moaned out the same thing from the pain and pleasure that she was feeling. "Look at me. Look at me girl," I commanded her.

Courtney looked at me and made me instantly fall in love with her. If I wasn't sure then, I was damn sure that I was in love with her now. I didn't want to be with any other woman or be a player no more. I wanted to be a man and show her a real love that didn't hurt her or keep her locked up in the house. She looked at me and then she turned her head away, but I could tell that she was terrified. She was afraid of love and what it could do to her. Courtney was so used to protecting her heart and running away from love, but I wasn't going to let her get away from me. I grabbed her by her chin and made her look straight at me.

"Don't pull up on me."

"Mmkay," she said before she tried to look away again.

"I love you girl and I'm not a man that you can deny. You gon let me love you and provide for you whenever I feel like it. Ya feel me?" I asked her.

She looked at me like I was speaking a foreign language to her and I knew that she was ready to pop off on me, so I sped up my strokes and kissed her long and hard.

"Uuummm! Um," she moaned.

"Tell me what you want. Tell me what you want."

"I ain't never wanted nothing. I never wanted much of nothing except to be happy. I've always been afraid to accept the help of a man. They say that once you take something from a man or give him some coochie, then he thinks that he can control you and that he owns you. I'll get it on my own or go without before I take a handout from any man. That's on my life," she told me.

"Naw, never that cause I ain't never wanted nothing either. Look, I don't want nothing from you, but that's why you've got me. That's why I'm in your life. Look at me girl.

You're so precious. I'm a man that realizes what I've got. I don't want nobody else. I don't need nothing else except you in my life. Forever ridin by my side. I swear, I'mma give you the life that you deserve. I'll try my best to give you the world. Bae?" I asked to get her attention. "Believe me. I'mma give dem a reason to hate you shawty," I told her.

"Just love me Adric."

Courtney placed her hands around my neck and brought her body closer to my chest.

"Girl, what you doing?" I asked her with a puzzled look on my face.

She leaned her body forward and scooted her ass up towards my groin area to put that pussy on me.

"I- I- I," I stuttered.

"You what?" she asked me as she whined her hips and came down on my dick.

"I don't wanna share you wit nobody else. You better not give my pussy away." I grabbed her around her neck, kissed her, and stared deep inside her eyes. "We finna go get you a test and make you a doctor appointment cause I'll go crazy if you pregnant by that fuck nigga," I told her.

"Who Jeremiah?" she asked me.

"Any nigga," I pushed her back on the bed and made love to her like the world was bout to end.

I watched her sleep like a baby and started to regret the fact that I was keeping a secret from her.

"Marry me," I whispered in her ear before I got up from her bed to dip out on her lil ass again. "FUCK!" I screamed as I drove to Teamber's townhouse that I'd bought for her.

19

Jeremiah

I was livid just seeing this nigga park his car at Courtney's crib, but I was going to wait it out to see how long he stayed in there with her. I didn't understand why and how she kept allowing herself to fuck with this punk ass nigga Slade. A real man wouldn't share his woman with his friends no matter the circumstance. I just wanted to ask her one question. I wanted to know why she keep going back to him. I wanted to know why she kept letting that nigga back in.

My emotions were getting the best of me and I knew how bad he treated her sometimes, so I got out my car because she needed someone to be there to protect her. I was walking across the street to her building when I noticed AD getting out of his car and walking up to her apartment door to knock. Someone came to the door, so I was wondering who the fuck else was in there with her.

I punched the air and turned around to walk back to my car cause I had to get the fuck up out of there before I snapped. I drove home and chilled at the house for an hour before I thought about the girl that I'd met at the club last night. I searched through my phone to call her to see if she wanted to go out with me to get something to eat. Mya agreed, so I rolled up two blunts of loud and placed them back inside of the foil package before I checked my messages to see if she'd texted me her address like I'd asked her to. I walked up to her apartment door to greet her, opened the car door for her, and drove us to the Huddle House.

"I like the Waffle House better," Mya complained when I parked my car inside of the vacant parking spot.

That was strike one for me because I needed someone by my side that could appreciate the little things in life. I didn't have to feed her or even offer to take her out anywhere, but I did it because I wanted to spend some time to get to know her and see what she was all about. I ignored the lil petty comments and shady shit that she was saying throughout the time that we spent in the booth together, but I knew that I was cutting shorty off as soon as I dropped her back off at her house.

I paid for our dinner and then I let her get her own door once we walked out of the restaurant. She had her face so deep in her phone that she didn't even notice the change in my attitude and demeanor. She didn't acknowledge the simple things that I did for her, so I knew that she was someone that I couldn't spend the rest of my life with. I was driving when my phone started to ring.

"Hello? Who this?" I asked the caller on the other end of the line.

"It's Slade fuck nigga!"

"DA FUCK YOU CALLIN MY PHONE FOR?" The veins in my neck flexed so hard at the sound of this nigga's voice. "What you doing going over Courtney's house for? Huh? I nutted all up in that pussy and stroked my shit so deep up in her cervix, so ain' no need for you to be taking yo ass over there," I told him.

"PULL UP ON ME NIGGA!" he challenged me like I wasn't a street nigga that would accept the challenge.

"THIS AIN'T WHAT THE FUCK YOU WANT! SHIT, I GOT ONE UP ON YOU NOW BRO," I laughed. "I've been waiting to plant my seed up in ha. Yo bitch. The bitch bad. I did that shit on purpose. I can't wait to find out if Courtney's pregnant and if I'mma be a daddy," I told him.

"WHAT?" Mya screamed.

I'd honestly forgotten that she was in the car with me when I was talking shit to Paiton.

"I'm done with the talkin. Pull up on me and run me my one," he told me.

"BET. I'm on the way nigga," I said to him before I turned my attention back to her.

"My, my bad Mya," I started before she put her hand up and cut me off.

"TAKE ME HOME JEREMIAH. YOU SICK! I can't believe that you'd try and play me like that. You been fuckin another bitch and tryna get her pregnant. What the hell you thought was gon happen between you and me? Lose my number. Don't call me no mo," she said.

"You ungrateful anyway. I wasn't calling you no more after I dropped you off Mya. Your standards too high for a nigga of my caliber. It was a test and you failed it hoe," I said through my laugher.

"Mmmhuh. Whatever. You just didn't want me to diss you or cut you off first." I watched her fold her arms across her chest and turn her nose up like she was the shit or like a nigga needed her.

"Naw. I was tryna see if you could appreciate the simple things, but you expected too much from me on our first date. It don't matter if it's McDonalds or a five-star restaurant, you should've been appreciative of anything that you wasn't having to pay for," I schooled her and stopped the car right in front of her apartment building. "Get out of my car," I told her.

I was hoping that I'd never have to see Mya again and sparked up one of the blunts to calm my nerves before I pulled up on Slade to see about that noise that he was talking. I jumped out of my car as soon as I saw him and ran up on him. I cocked my arm back after hearing him disrespect me, talking bout he'd kill Courtney and the baby if he found out that she was carrying my seed, and got knocked the fuck back cause that nigga was too quick wit it.

I wasn't no bitch for a nigga, so I gave that pussy ass nigga this work until we ended up on the ground, throwing blows, and cursing each other out. Finally, the nigga reached around his back and pulled out his pistol to point it in my face.

"Pow!"

Fuck, the nigga had hit me, but I was losing consciousness fast. I didn't know what the fuck was going on around me, so I started praying to God. I prayed that I left a legacy behind to keep my name going. My eyes were getting heavy as shit and I couldn't keep my eyelids open, but all I could see was her, Courtney. I was blaming it on the effect of the weed that I'd just smoked, but then again, I knew that I was bleeding out. I could hear all the commotion surrounding me and folks crying out to call the police. I drew in a sharp breath and closed my eyes cause there was no point in me fighting this shit. This was my end.

20

Slade

Adric coming over to Courtney's house and kicking me and Britin out really was enough to make me set her whole apartment complex on fire. I was sick and tired of my bitch acting like she was a dog and doing shit out of spite like she was a motherfuckin nigga. Courtney never saw the love that I had for her and she couldn't get it through that thick skull of hers that she just couldn't be on the same shit that us niggas be on. A man couldn't carry and birth a baby and a woman couldn't do things that required the strength of a man.

The icing on the cake was the fact that my partner had done fucked my bitch and told me that he was tryna have a baby with her. I opened that door to let him be intimate with her, but I didn't expect for him to even want Courtney like that. Me and my niggas went for the baddest of bitches, but I chose Courtney to be my main bitch cause she was down to earth and regular as shit. She could do both. She could dress up and be a bad bitch with her nose up in the air or she could be cool as fuck and kick the bullshit with my people. It was fucked up, but it was a double standard when it came down to a man and woman's relationship.

I'd called Jeremiah cause he was my boy and I wasn't giving Courtney up for shit, so he was gonna have to fall back from her and tell her to get an abortion if she turned up pregnant by him. He wasn't going for that and then he had the nerve to try me like I was some lame ass fuck nigga that worked under him. I told him to pull up on me and say that shit to my face with his chest since he wanted to pop shit on the phone like he was bout it, bout it. Shit, we was gon see what the fuck he was talkin bout when he hit that pavement in the projects.

I continued serving them packs and talking big shit with my niggas them until I heard the tires screech in the hood. Everybody turned their heads to see who the hell was pulling up in the hood like that, but I knew to fuckin laugh at this clown ass nigga. Jeremiah got out his car wit the shit, so I matched his energy to prove to him that I was ready.

"Run me my one!" I said to him before he reached his arm back to knock the wind out of me. "Step the fuck down. You were my motherfuckin nigga." I reacted and punched him dead in his shit cause he'd let pussy get in the way of our brotherhood.

"You shouldn't have never let me hit yo bitch! I can't wait for you to watch me raise a kid witcho kept bitch nigga," he laughed in my face.

We were on the ground punching each other and fighting like we were getting paid for a televised boxing match. That shit right there, that last sentence that he said to me was the straw that broke the camel's back, and I just lost it. I reached behind my back and pulled out my pistol.

"I'll kill her and that fuckin baby before I watch you be wit her!" I told him.

"Adric over there in her guts anyway fuck nigga. She ain' gon choose you. You heard the way she was moaning when I was drilling a hole in her pussy," Jeremiah smirked and then I pointed my gun right up to his face.

"Pow!" my gun went off and his brain matter splattered all over my face.

The whole hood started screaming and my boys were shocked as fuck, but they knew what the fuck to do. One of them older grandmas had done called the fuckin police, so I heard sirens wailing in the background. I didn't regret a damn thing cause I didn't want to see nobody else with her. My thoughts were always on doing whatever it took to keep her in my grasp whether it was pulling up on her whenever she called me or splurging on her and buying her unnecessary shit.

I climbed off the nigga and used the end of my shirt to wipe his blood and pieces of his brain off my face, but it was so much blood and brain matter on me. I stood up on my feet and looked up at the crowd that was surrounding me. I watched Britin and Daisha both push through the crowd trying to get to me, but I wasn't in the mood to deal with none of their sobbing. I'd just shot a nigga over another bitch, but they weren't going to get the big picture.

"SLADE! SLADE!" Daisha ran over to me first. "I'm pregnant. Slade, we made a baby," she cried.

"Man, that baby ain' mines!" I said right before Britin rushed inside of my chest to hug me.

"Slade! What did you do? Slade, please. Say it ain't yours. You did this to me!" she cried hysterically.

"WHERE THE FUCK IS MY BRO? MAN, WHERE THE FUCK IS MY LIL BRO?" I scanned the crowd for Khari and the lil nigga was standing right on the side of me the entire time.

"That's foul what you did Paiton bro. You fucked my bitch and got her pregnant. You could have had any hoe you wanted, but you chose mines bro. Ain't no love lost Slade. Just know that karma gon be cold as fuck to ya," he told me.

"POLICE! PUT YOUR HANDS UP WHERE WE CAN SEE THEM! PUT EM UP, RIGHT NOW!" the officers screamed and yelled at me. "DROP THE GUN!" they instructed me.

I allowed the gun to fall out of my hands and hit the ground before I raised my hands up in the air.

"Goodbye," I murmured to anyone that could hear me.

21

Khari

This nigga here, I thought to myself.

It was fucked up how a street nigga would kill his day one over some pussy. I turned around and gave Daisha the mean mug cause I knew I wasn't tripping when I heard Daisha tell my brother that she was pregnant by him. Hell, I knew it wasn't my baby, so I wasn't feeding into the lie that Slade was telling when he said that Daisha wasn't pregnant by him. I was enraged, and it was fucked up how Daisha loved my brother more than she loved me. She'd do more for him than she'd do for me because we strapped up every time that we fucked, but she let that nigga hit it raw on the first night.

I was questioning myself, tryna come up with a timeline to figure out if they'd been fucking on the low and trying not to lose my mind. I couldn't stop the tears from falling from my eyes as I ran to my car while the police placed my brother in handcuffs. I didn't have nobody to talk to, so I got inside of my car and drove straight to her house. Courtney.

She was always a good listening ear, and I could call her about anything. Most of the time I called her just to hear her voice and to vent to her because she was a real down ass bitch that gave me sound advice. Courtney told me the shit that I didn't want to hear, and she didn't back down from me whenever I disagreed with her.

I cried the entire drive to her house, parked my car, and ran up to her apartment door. I pounded my fists against her door, hoping that she was at home, and that no one had told her the news of Slade getting locked up before I could tell her. It was hard as fuck watching my brother get locked up behind her.

"Who is it?" she asked me from behind the door.

"It's Khari! Courtney, open the door!" I begged her.

"Okay, okay. What's up?" I looked at her and could tell that either she'd been asleep or getting fucked.

I told her what happened and that she was the reason behind Slade shooting Jeremiah, but she didn't want to hear it. She shook her head in disbelief, but it was true. My brother loved her the most out of all his hoes. Courtney took a few steps to let me inside of her apartment and then I told her that my girl Daisha had gotten knocked up by my brother. I didn't want to tell her that Daisha was pregnant by my brother cause it just wouldn't have sounded right. My ex-girlfriend was having a baby with my brother who was going to prison for murder. I placed my hands on her shoulders and looked her straight in her eyes.

"Courtney, Daisha and Slade are about to have a child together. She just told him after he shot Jeremiah, but he says the baby isn't his. I know for a fact that it ain't mines."

"I can't. I can't deal with that shit no more. I don't care. I DON'T FUCKING CARE!" she yelled. Her voice cracked, and tears fell from her eyes. I knew that shit had to hurt her and that it was killing her inside. "Don't come telling me nothing else about him. Khari, you'll always be like a lil brother to me, but you can't keep running to me, telling me everything about your brother, and imposing on my life. You can call me if you need to talk. As for me and your brother, it's over between us," she told me.

I could tell that this time she was serious about being done with my bro, because for as long as I'd known Courtney, she was always there for the both of us. If we couldn't count on no one else, we could count on her. I nodded my head to let her know that I understood where she was coming from with this shit.

"Okay sis. Stay up in life and I'll call you once a month," I told her before I released my hand from her shoulder and went for a hug.

Courtney hugged me and wiped the tears that were on her face. I was hurting inside myself, too, but I tried to smile for her because she was gonna be alright. Paiton had really fucked her up, but better days were coming for her because she had that nigga Adric in her life, so I knew that he would show her a different lifestyle than the one that my brother had shown her.

I walked out of her house and booked myself a flight on my iPhone. Somebody had to run the family business and control the streets, and Daisha had awakened the savage inside of me.

"Fuck school," I said aloud as I got inside of my car and drove home to pack a traveling bag to fly to Cuba and inform my father of Slade's misfortune.

I cried and got in my feelings once I arrived at me and Slade's house cause I was in the house alone for the first time since we'd moved in that bitch together. My phone started ringing off the hook, so I had to silence the ringer. I looked at my screen and saw my father's name scroll across my lock screen, so I answered for him.

"Pops!" I exclaimed.

"I heard about your brother. I need for you to be all in. Come home and learn the ropes of this business," he told me.

"I fly out tomorrow," I confirmed.

"Good, good. I'll have a car waiting for you at the airport," KP said before the phone line went dead.

I knew one thing was for sure; I was going to come back to Atlanta and make a name for myself. A bitch was the furthest thing on my mind. I was paper chasing all year long. I went to bed and woke up with Paiton on my mind and, even though he was wrong, he was still my blood and my brother. I told myself that I was gonna put something on his commissary account and visit him when I got back. I stopped by Verizon Wireless and changed my number, and then I drove to the airport to fly out.

22

Mya

I wasn't sweating no nigga cause these niggas were like spare change. You'd always find a penny lying around somewhere. They came a dime a dozen, so Jeremiah could go on and start a family with her. I was wishing that I knew who the fuck this Courtney bitch was, so I could compare myself to her. I was trying my hardest to act like I didn't give a damn that he'd just said that shit in front of me like I wasn't listening or paying attention to him. Jeremiah had taken me to the Huddle House like I was some ratchet bitch and then he had the nerve to tell someone that he was talking to on the phone that Adric was over her house… that damn Courtney bitch. All I've ever wanted was a nigga that could take me away from my problems, but Khari didn't want me and Adric had yet to call me.

"Who the hell is this Courtney bitch? What does she have over me?" I asked myself.

I went to bed hoping that I'd be able to put this shit behind me, but it was killing me to know that he was trying to start a family with some other local bitch. I woke up to my phone ringing nonstop, so I looked at the caller ID to see who it was, and why my phone was buzzing back to back like that. It was my homegirls, so I knew that they must've had some piping hot tea to tell me. I answered the phone and then my friend said that we should do a video chat through the Facebook Messenger app. I was curious to know why these hoes were blowing up my phone, so I gave them a look that said, *"What?"*

"You need to get yo ass over here to the hood!" one of my girls said. She flipped her camera and showed me how hot the block was.

"Damn, erybody out!" I squealed. "What's going on over there? A cookout or something? Adric over there?" A big smile spread across my face cause he was fine as fuck and paid. Plus, I wanted him for myself since this Courtney chick was talking to him on the low.

My friends ignored me, so I knew that the people that were out weren't hanging out for no celebration.

"Wasn't you wit Jeremiah last night?" my girl asked me.

"Yeah, what's that? What? What's wrong?" I sat up in my bed and felt my heart drop to my stomach. "Is he alright?" I gulped and swallowed my gathered saliva.

"He just got shot," my other friend told me.

"Aaaahhh! No! What? Oh my God! Oh my God! I'm

on the way!" I tossed my phone and jumped up out of my bed to throw on something presentable to wear over there.

I brushed my teeth, brushed up my hair in a ponytail, and grabbed my car keys, so that I could rush out the door. I was worrying myself sick all the way over there. I was hoping that he was okay because my girls had told me that he'd been shot. They didn't say that he was in critical condition or dead. I pulled up to the projects just in time to see his body being loaded on the gurney. I rushed over to him and tried to look at him, but I was pushed back by two police officers. My eyes grew wide and I collapsed to the ground with tears flowing from my eyes onto my cheeks. He wasn't alive. He was dead when I reached him.

I felt like I couldn't win for losing. I wanted to change his mind about me even though he thought that I had high standards. I still wanted to get to know Jeremiah even though he wanted a family with her. I was hurt because I'd lost the man that I knew loved me without a shadow of a doubt behind fucking with Khari and then Jeremiah came along and gave me some kind of hope. I wanted to love again and to find the right person, but it seemed like God was punishing me. I was being punished for what I did to Idris. I looked around the projects for Khari; he had to be here because his brother had just shot and murdered this man, but he wasn't in the projects. I listened to the gossip on what had just happened and found out that Slade had killed Jeremiah over this Courtney woman.

"What does she have that I don't have to make all these men sweat her? Why do they want her?" I asked myself aloud.

I had to find out more about this woman, so I asked around about her. Everybody said nice things about her, so I just listened, and continued asking questions. I found out where she lived at through a girl named Britin who was supposed to be a close friend of hers.

I got inside of my car and thought about how I'd given Adric my phone number inside of the club. How he went to her house to lay up and shit. Jeremiah knew, so that told me that he'd been peeping her and watching her, but Slade had shot Jeremiah over her. All three of these men really had feelings for and cared about this hoe. She must've had some good pussy, or she must've been paying them to fuck with her. Either way, I was about to pull up on her and see whose nigga she was fucking with now. All that was left for me was Khari, but I knew that right now he needed his space. I pulled up at the apartment complex where Courtney supposedly stayed. I noticed Khari walking out of the apartment building.

He'd driven to her house too, I thought when I noticed him coming out from the building where Britin said that she lived.

I couldn't stand the way that these men loved her ass, so I told myself that I was going to watch Courtney, too.

"I hate her, and I don't even know her!" I cried out in despair as I drove to my house.

The next day, Khari left the city, so I told myself that I was going to give him time to do whatever it was that he needed to do before I made my move. I planned to get in good with him and ask him questions about her, so that I could ruin this bitch's life. I hated her, and I didn't even know her at all.

23

Idris

My homeboy Adric called me early this morning, telling me that he needed to set up a meeting with me, and that he was interested in having me design a house for him. I entertained the idea and decided to meet up with him for dinner at a local restaurant here in the city. I arrived early because when I was younger someone told me that being on time was considered being late, so I arrived ten to thirty minutes early to every meeting that I had with people.

I was sitting at a table waiting for Adric to show up until I started to wonder where the hell the nigga was at. I looked at my watch on my left arm and back up at the door to see if he was walking through the door of the restaurant yet. A courtesy call would've been nice, yet he didn't send me a text or a phone call to let me know that he was running late. I told myself that I was going to wait five more minutes for him, and then I was going to get up and leave if he hadn't shown up. I looked down to look at the menu that sat in front of me and when I looked back up, I noticed Adric Hernandez walking towards the table. He was inconsiderate as fuck and late, but I still stood up to greet him like a businessman was supposed to.

"What's up man? Say, you late aintcha?" I asked him to let him know that I felt a way about him showing up ten minutes past the time that we'd scheduled for our sit down.

I reached my arm across the table to shake his hand, and then I proceeded to sit down.

"You know how these women are," Adric said to me.

I watched him closely while he pulled his chair and sat down at the table.

I sat down in my chair and got straight to it. "What can I do for you?" I asked him.

"I fell in love with a real one. The right one and she needs a house. To be honest, Courtney deserves that and much more."

I stared at Adric cause I'd never heard him talk like that throughout all the time that I'd known him.

"Alright then man. Let's draw up a blueprint. Do you have anything in mind on what you're looking for? Any specific details."

"She like simple things, so it shouldn't be too hard. She's an excellent swimmer, so I'm looking for a pool. I want to start off small, three or four bedrooms, and something under the price range of $500,000," he told me.

"Okay, I'll start looking around for a house that meets your needs then," I said to him. "I didn't even know that you were seeing anybody. How long y'all been together? This yo ex-girlfriend?" I asked him curiously.

"We just been coolin it," he laughed. "Naw, she ain't my ex. You asking too many questions aintcha?" he asked me.

I laughed before I responded to him. "I respect that. Let's get out of here, so I can go and get back with my girl," I confessed to Adric.

"Aight. Keep me updated with anything that you find." AD stood up from where he sat at the table and shook my hand.

I gave him a handshake and stood up to leave myself. I took my time walking out of the restaurant because I was my own boss and I didn't have to answer to anyone or punch nobody's clocks. I'd been watching Mya over the past two weeks to see if she was worth me taking back because we'd been together for a while and I was in love with her even though she did some fuck shit to piss me off and make me want to never see or speak to her again. I knew for a fact that Mya was out cheating on me when she didn't answer her phone for me and when that shit started going straight to voicemail.

I told myself that I had to get my bitch back after she went out to the club and started entertaining other niggas. Mya was a homebody and she never went out to the clubs like that, so I could tell that she was desperately trying to get over me. Adric had me thinking about my future now that he was taking a female serious, so I pulled out my phone and called Mya to see if we could meet up.

Mya answered the phone quick as fuck, so it made me feel good to know that she'd answer the phone for me whenever I called her. She wasn't easy to pull or impress, so I knew that I had to get her with the food. Mya wasn't big or nothing, but she had that happy weight on her cause she liked to eat. I knew how much she loved a good ass burnt hot dog and dippin' dots ice cream, so I started off the conversation by asking her if she'd eaten anything today.

Mya and I didn't get the chance to spend a lot of our time together, but I knew my woman. I was aware that she hadn't eaten anything because she didn't like to eat breakfast food. We agreed to meet up at her favorite hotdog stand, so I rushed there to be there by the time that she got there. Mya came walking towards me and I finally acknowledged the way that I felt about her. She stopped in front of me and said hey, but I'd missed the hell out of her, so I told her something that she wasn't expecting to hear from me.

"I'll take you back." I whispered in her ear when she hugged me.

She broke our embrace and took a step back to look at me.

"What's on your mind?" I asked her.

"This woman named Courtney," Mya told me.

"That name sounds familiar," I furrowed my eyebrows together and tried to think of where I'd heard that name before. "Oh!" I snapped my fingers together. "I'm drawing up a blueprint for her a house just in case I can't find her anything that's already been built," I told Mya as we walked towards the hot dog stand.

"Her what?"

"Her man wants me to prepare a house for her. You know what I do for a living. I'm an architect." I told her.

"Hmm," she moaned as we stopped in front of the hot dog stand to order our hotdogs.

I was standing there wondering how Mya knew Adric's girl. Adric hadn't mentioned much about her and I didn't want to ask Mya anything about her either. You know how these women are. They'd get offended when you ask them something about another woman and swear up and down that y'all had something going on. I wasn't looking for them problems right now. I just wanted to make things right between her and I.

Mya got her hot dog first and immediately started eating it before I got mines, but I didn't blame her because they were better when they were fresh. I grabbed mines from the stand attendant and walked with her to a nearby bench, so that we could sit down and talk. Mya and I talked out our differences and then we tried to pretend like we were interested in the dippin dots' ice cream when we were really only interested in getting back to my crib so we could fuck.

"You want some ice cream?" I asked Mya. I loved the way she stared at me and licked her lips before she looked down at my dick. "Aight. Come on then." I tossed my hot dog container in the trash can before I removed the carton that her hotdog had been in from her hand to do the same thing with it.

"Where are you taking me?" she asked.

"Girl, you always got a million and one questions to ask somebody. You can't never let a nigga surprise you," I laughed. "I ought to fuck you in the car, but I miss the fuck outta you, so you finna take it all." I grinned from ear to ear.

"But what about my car? What are we gonna do about my car? We can't just leave it sitting here!"

"Like hell we can. You trust daddy?" I stopped walking and let go of her hand to look at her.

It was that moment there that I knew my bitch was a slut, but she was my slut. Didn't no other woman have my heart the way that she had it. I can't tell you what it was about her that intrigued me, but I was going to let her know what it was one more time and that was gonna be it. I didn't have to wait around for her to get right and I wanted her to know that. I'm a man with many options, so she could learn how to be faithful and respect me or find another nigga, but nan' nigga could compare to me. I knew the type of man that she wanted and needed in her life and we were slim to none out here in Atlanta. Even if she did find another nigga of my caliber, he wouldn't be faithful like me.

"I trust you," she told me.

"Alright. I'm gon bring you back to your car once we're done or get somebody to bring it over to my house. You must have forgotten who the fuck I am?" I asked her to remind her who she was fucking with.

"No-no. Idris! Do you have to say that?" She looked around to make sure that nobody heard me ask her that.

"Shit. Seems like you forgot. I was just asking. Come on baby."

I led the way to my car and opened the passenger door so Mya could get in. We talked and tried our best to catch up on the way to my house, but neither one of us could keep our hands off each other during the drive. I parked my car and walked around to open her door for her. I could tell that she missed a nigga and my dick couldn't resist the urge to poke out at the sight of her. I opened the passenger door and waited for her to turn towards me to get out of the car before I pushed her back against the armrest and the driver seat.

"I can't wait. I've got to have you! I need to feel you," I confessed to Mya as I undid the buttons on her jeans.

She leaned her head back and allowed me to remove her pants before she let out a loud shriek when I entered inside of her pussy.

"IDRIS!" she screamed.

"You missed me?"

"Mmmhhhmmm!" she moaned as she lifted her legs to place them by my sides to grant me greater access inside of her.

I fucked her for two minutes before I picked her up and carried her inside of my house. I didn't give a fuck that we were half dressed and half naked cause I just wanted her. I opened the house door and ran up the staircase of my house, pumping inside of her, and staring at her to let her know the love was real between me and her. Any other man wouldn't have taken her back for the shit that she did, but I was really in love with her hoe ass. But still I had to get this shit off my chest and let her know just how much I loved the fuck out of her. My heart was hers and I loved her so much that I didn't want no one else to have her at all. I covered her body with mine and let out a moan while I kissed her along the side of her face and ears.

"If I see you wit that nigga ever again.... I'mma kill the both of y'all." I leaned upright and gently choked Mya while I sped up my strokes.

"OH! Okay baby," she moaned before she squirted her juices against my pubic hairs.

"Okay, what?" I released the grip that I had on her neck to kiss her and stare deeply into her eyes.

"You won't see me with him ever again." Mya threw her head back and pointed her toes to the ceiling while I was digging deep inside her.

"Good. Now, tell me what I want to hear." I used my hands to hold her calves up higher.

"I love you Idris," she leaned her body forward and whispered into my ear.

"I love you too girl," I told her before I came and fell on top of her breasts to fall asleep.

24

Daisha

All I heard was commotion and people screaming, "They fighting! They fighting! FIGHT!"

"Who's fighting?" I asked a girl that was standing beside me, but she stared at me and rolled her eyes.

I didn't know what this chick's beef was with me, but I ain' even know her like that for her to be turning up her nose and rolling her eyes at me. A part of me wanted to snatch this hoe up and put this work on her, but I had a baby to live for. I hadn't told Slade yet because I knew what he'd say. I was his brother's girlfriend, so it would look real suspicious if I popped up pregnant by him and delivered his baby in nine months.

I walked towards the crowd and suddenly my heart stopped. It was the father of my unborn child fighting this nigga Jeremiah. I hoped to God that they weren't fighting over that bitch that had participated in that foursome that we had at his house. I didn't regret a thing that happened that night because I was for sure that I'd gotten pregnant during our first encounter. Tears flooded my eyes as I watched him reach behind him to pull out his gun.

"Nnnoooo! SLADE! Stop!" I screamed as I pushed through the crowd and ran over to him. "I'm pregnant," I whispered.

It was too late because he'd already shot him. The girl that was looking at me like I was crazy was standing there professing her love for him and talking out the side of her neck, but I was bout to burst her bubble. I heard the sirens wailing in the distance, so it was now or never, but I had to tell him.

"I'M PREGNANT!" I blurted out in front of all those people.

"Man, that baby ain' mines!" he yelled at me.

I was embarrassed, so I said all that I could say to him to let him know that I was telling the truth. It wasn't like we'd only fucked one time on some booty call shit. The whole hood saw us leave together just the other day, so I guess I had to remind the nigga.

"We made a baby," I said with a raised eyebrow.

This bitch that was standing beside me had the nerve to question my pussy. I remembered her. She was Courtney's best friend, so I was tryna figure out why the fuck she cared so much if it was true or not. *"They fuckin,"* I said to myself. Slade looked at me, but I knew that look because he'd looked at me like that before. He couldn't deny his feelings for me even if he wanted to and I knew it was wrong, but somehow, I just fell for him. He was everything that I didn't want my man to be, and he was my ex-boyfriend's brother. Now, I'm standing here trying to keep a smile on my face as I watch him be handcuffed like he's a fucking animal. All I wanted to do was scream at the police officers and run to him to feel his touch one last time before they took him away from me.

I turned my back to him and walked in the direction of my mama's house while I cried and ignored the talk and stares from the other girls that lived here in the hood. I was worried, thinking that I'd never see him again, and thinking crazy thoughts.

"Should I keep his child that's growing inside of me?" I kept asking myself.

There was no way that Slade could plead self-defense or say that he accidently shot his friend, so I knew that they were finna lock him away from me and our kid for a long ass time. I closed my eyes and wiped at the tears that were rolling down my face. I pushed the door hard as fuck cause I was angry at myself for letting this happen. If I had of been there, then Slade would've seen my face and never shot Jeremiah. I kept thinking of all the shit that I could've done to prevent him from making the biggest mistake of his life. My mama looked at me like she was ready to fuss and say something bout the way that I'd pushed her door open and let it slam behind me, so I gave her that look that dared her to say something.

Surprisingly, she didn't say anything, but I was just tired. I felt like I could go to sleep, wake up, and go back to sleep. I'd just found out that I was pregnant today, and I kept having to eat on some ice or chew some gum to keep the saliva from gathering inside of my mouth. I couldn't stop fucking craving shit, burping, spitting, and wanting to sleep. I was so nauseated and sleepy that it didn't make no sense.

I should've known that I was pregnant because I was ready to cry any time my mama said one word to me that offended me. I walked inside of the kitchen and searched through the cabinets for some liquor. I didn't want to go through with this and keep this nigga's baby. My biggest fear was having to raise this child on my own because it was unfair as fuck. Life was always unkind to me and I never got to move up out of the projects and have my happy ending. Why did I have to go through this? Why did I have to live like this? I didn't want to feel anything, so I poured myself up a cup of liquor.

"Maybe this will kill you," I told my unborn as I tossed back the cup of liquor and grimaced from the alcohol burning my throat.

I went inside of my bedroom and crashed on my bed after my head started spinning from the effect of the alcohol. My mama came knocking on my room door a few hours later, but I didn't want to move. I felt so queasy and I knew that if I moved, then I was going to throw up everywhere. My stomach was touching my back, and I was starving myself and my baby. Being lovesick hurt like hell, but I couldn't eat if I didn't hear from him. Paiton "Slade" Perez was like my drug, and I was his junkie. I didn't have an appetite if I didn't take a hit or have a dose of him.

"COME IN!" I said with anger in my voice.

"You've got to eat baby," my mama said to me.

"Why? Because I'm pregnant? Or because I'm a skinny ass fuck up?" I cried and covered my hand over my mouth to stop from vomiting all over myself, but it was too late.

"SHIT! GIRL! You've got to learn how to keep a trash

Give Them A Reason to Hate You Shawty

can beside your bed until your nausea symptoms go away. How far along are you anyway?" she asked me.

"I'm four weeks," I confessed to her.

"Oh, that was fast. You and Khari are going to make great parents' baby. Is he excited?"

I broke down crying as my phone started ringing. "It's not his baby mama! It's his...It's his brother's baby. I've been fucking Slade and I'm in love with him, but now he's gone!" I shouted hysterically.

"Oh no! You've got to get rid of it! I'm not going to have you out here making me look like an unfit mother. Like I raised some hooker hoe. Oh, no! No ma'am. YOU KNEW BETTER DAISHA! Fix it Jesus!" she yelled. "Your ass better make your appointment to abort that bastard tomorrow," my mama said.

I looked down at my phone and swiped my finger across the home screen to answer. I didn't know who it was calling me this late in the evening, because my shit was always so fucking dry. I didn't have many friends and the ones that I had were jealous of me because of how Slade had picked me over them the other day on the block.

They just didn't know the type of dick this nigga had. It was like his dick had superpowers to make a girl see nobody else or nothing else except for him. You'd be left craving him and wondering what the fuck he was doing or where he was at when he wasn't with you. I placed the phone to my ear and listened to a bunch of chatter and background noise.

"Hello? Daisha? Are you there?"

My heart melted, and I felt flutters inside of my stomach, so I giggled and smiled for the first time that day.

"Slade...."

"Yeah, I'm here. I just wanted to call you and ask you. Were you for real? You having a nigga baby?" he asked me.

"I thought that you'd call someone else and that I'd be a distant memory to you. Thought that you'd forget about me," I cried. "Yes, I'm pregnant, but you made it clear. You don't want the baby, so I'm going to get rid of it tomorrow." I sniffled to keep my tears from flowing, but I broke down crying on the phone with him.

That shit hurt me that he would deny me and act like I never meant nothing to him. He pushed me away and left me looking stupid in front of everybody, so it was hard for me to sit on the phone and listen to him. *Why is he calling me?* I asked myself.

"I loved you since the first night that you let me hit it. How could I forget you? I didn't strap up with you on purpose. Keep my baby. Take care of my seed. Do that for me," Slade said to me.

"Slade. I've gotta- I've gotta go," I rushed off the phone with him and cried myself to sleep because I was undecided.

A part of me wanted to keep this baby to always have a piece of him with me and the other part of me wanted to run back to Khari and ask him for his forgiveness. His brother wasn't going to be able to be a part of our child's life, so there was no point in me birthing this child. Plus, I'm still young myself and I got my own life to live.

I silenced my phone and drifted off to sleep with thoughts of suicide running through my mind. I knew that my mama would kick me out on my ass if she found out that I'd kept this baby after she told me to make an appointment, and she damn sure wasn't about to let any letters from Slade come to her mailbox, so I woke up and made my appointment. I had to cover myself up with a jacket like I was a celebrity when I walked out of the house to get inside of my mama's car. These folks in the hood were nosey as fuck. I broke down and looked down at my stomach when my mama's car pulled up in front of the abortion clinic.

"MA! Don't make me do it! I don't want to do it!" I waved my hands up in the air frantically as I talked to her.

"YOU'RE YOUNG AND YOU HAVE YOUR WHOLE LIFE AHEAD OF YOU! Trust me. Trust mama. It's for the best. I'll be right there with you. I'mma be right beside you. It won't hurt too bad," she convinced me.

I went inside of the clinic, filled out the paperwork, and kept running to the bathroom until they called me back to take the life that was growing inside of me out of me. I didn't feel much, but the little twinge of pain that I did feel from the suction made me want to jump up off the operation table. My abortion made me not want to have sex again for a long time, and it hurt worse than I could ever imagine. Emotionally and mentally is where it hurt the most.

Slade called me once I got home, and I locked myself inside of my room. I hated him so much for getting me pregnant and then doing some stupid shit where he'd have to go away and leave me to raise a child on my own. I always thought that he'd be the one to take me away from here and show me something different. Give me the life that I deserved, but he was no different than these other dumb ass, fake hustling niggas.

"Don't call me again, Slade. Forget that you ever met me," I told him before I hung up the phone.

I was going to make it out of this hood on my own. *Fuck a nigga,* I thought. I just wanted to be alone until I bounced back from this depression that I was experiencing.

25

Britin

I couldn't stand the thought of another woman having Slade's baby. I've been trying to come up with a timeline on when he had the time to fuck another bitch and get her pregnant ever since they came and locked him up. My heart still wanted him, but my mind knew what I had to motherfuckin do. I had to boss up on that nigga and make him want me and only me. I was so tired of fucking sharing him with my lame ass friend and now, this young ass hoe thought that a baby was gonna keep him wrapped around her fingers. Uh uhn, not the Slade that I knew. He told her the right motherfuckin thing. He'd better know the next time that I ask him.

"Was the child his?" I kept pondering. *"And why this nigga ain't called me yet?"* I wondered as I packed up my shit.

I was hopeful that they were going to let my baby out on bail and that he'd need some good lovin before he was sentenced. I was gon be the bitch that was right there with a place for him to stay and some good sex. For Courtney to be my friend, she damn sure hadn't called me since the incident. That was weird because she should've wanted to vent and complain about how this man had done had a baby on her and how he went out bad shooting his day one over her homebody ass.

"I bet he's been using all his minutes to call her," I mumbled as I loaded up my small, white Nissan Sentra. That was alright cause I was going to ride over to her house to throw it up in her face that a bitch was moving on up like the Jefferson's. I ran over to the driver's side of my car to look inside at my phone to make sure that I hadn't missed his phone call, but the nigga still hadn't hit my line yet.

"What the fuck is taking him so long to call me?" I asked myself aloud before I slammed my car door.

I went back inside of my mama's apartment to grab a few small items that I could sit on my passenger seat and on my backseat before I hugged her and told her that I'd call her before I went to sleep.

"Drive safe. Be careful, and make sure you lock your doors good behind you once you get in," she told me.

"Aight ma, dang. I ain't no baby," I fussed.

I closed her house door and rushed to my car. I was

itching to flex and boast in front of Courtney. Slade had shown her how to get it on her own, and the nigga had initially moved her out of the hood, so I was in my feelings because he never had the chance to do the same damn thing for me. I was in a secret competition with her, because she always got everything that she wanted without even asking a nigga for it. I couldn't stand her. I opened my car door to see my LED light flashing on my phone, so I picked it up quick. It was an unknown number, so I answered the phone.

"*Let it be him. Please, let it be him,*" I prayed before I answered the phone. "Who is this?" I asked the caller on the other end of the phone.

"That's how you answer yo phone," he checked me.

I always got wet from the sound of his voice, but his cologne and the way that he could go and spend a check on some Versace, or some expensive shit is what really turned me on. I'd been watching Slade since he was a young nigga coming up under his father's workers. It damn near killed me when he chose Courtney over me. I always wondered what was wrong with me, and why he chose the weak bitch to be his main bitch. He really loved her, though, but I wanted him to see me for once.

"Whatchu want?" I snapped like I was mad at him. "Why are you calling my phone?" I asked him.

"You've always been the one. You've always had my heart. You gon ride for me?"

He'd finally said the things that I'd been waiting for him to say to me for a long time, but I wasn't moved by that shit at all.

"Sslllaaddeee!" I hummed into the phone.

"What's it gonna be girl?" he asked me. "You gon ride for daddy?"

"Hmm. Why it took you so long to ask me? Huh?" I

smiled hard as fuck through my sentences because I was just happy that he finally noticed that I was his rider.

"Mmm. Yeen sayin nothin." I ignored his complaints because I wasn't ready to answer him just yet.

I wanted the nigga to hear about the moves that I was making, so that he'd want to come home to me and be the motherfuckin boss for me. Shit, he'd given this bitch a whole fairy tale dream for them not to even be together anymore. Last I heard, Courtney was fucking a nigga who had more money and street cred than Slade had, so you know what I wanted. I wanted everything that was hers. I wanted to be spoiled and fucking on a nigga with long money, but I had to start with the peon first. I promised myself that I'd finesse the fuck out of Paiton first and then I'd move on to take Adric away from Courtney. I had to outdo her because I was never her real friend to begin with.

"You still there?" he asked me.

"Mmhuh. What's up? How they treatin you in there?" I asked him.

"You know me. I'm surviving. I'm forever straight and good. This jail shit's like a walk in the park for me. She killed my baby man. She killed my baby!" he said, frustrated.

"So, that motherfucker was yours? Really, Slade? But you say you love me though?" My heart broke and shattered inside of my chest.

"How could he do this to me? And then he had the nerve to ask me to ride for him? Like I was second best, when he couldn't even keep his dick in his pants while he was out here?" I asked myself.

"I don't know! Damn it, man. I don't know. You know I love you. It was an accident," he lied.

"YOU MOTHERFUCKING LYING CAUSE THE

WHOLE HOOD KNOW SHE FOLLOWED YOU HOME THE OTHER DAY! THAT'S WHY I'M MOVING AWAY!" I screamed as I pounded my fists against my steering wheel and poked my chest into the horn. "HELL NO! I'm not! I'm not ridin for you! Got me out here looking fucking stupid!" I yelled.

I was so fucking irritated with how he thought he was finna play me. Niggas always wanted to come back around when they had to do some serious time and hold a bitch's life up. My heart wanted to be there for him, but my mind screamed, no. I was always available to him, yet he was playing games with me for my best friend. The bitch didn't even want him the way that I wanted him, and she damn sure couldn't fuck him like I fucked him. This young hoe, his baby mama, she had some sense about her though. She got rid of his baby and moved the fuck on, so I told myself that I had to get off the phone and pull up on Courtney. I needed to get close to big daddy Adric. He'd checked me and told me that I couldn't get the dick, so I was looking at him as my new person of interest.

"Calm down girl. You know I love you," Slade told me.

"Uh uhn. Nigga, you'n love me. You want me to be down for you while you do them years in prison, and I ain't finna be waiting around on you when there's other men out here that'll love and claim me. A nigga that won't fucking lie to me and be out here fuckin this bitch and that bitch. A man that'll choose me first before he even get with my best friend. Courtney was dumb for your ass, but I'm smarter than that bitch. That's why yo dumb ass never chose me from the beginning cause you knew that I wasn't gon have none of that. Bye Slade. I'm glad that girl killed your baby. Fuck you," I cried to him.

He was every girl's fantasy, and bitches stayed wanting to holla bout how they were fuckin with him, so I couldn't help but to want him until he tried to play me like I was the one to be played with. I wanted to get home, take a shower, and unload my car, so I drove to my apartment to get some of this shit out of my car, and then I crashed on my air mattress.

I was living in an apartment in Dunwoody. It was out of my price range, but I told myself that I'd find me a sugar daddy on one of these websites within the next three months. I was willing to do anything to not go back to my mama's house. I was stirring on the uncomfortable ass, wobbly, unstable air mattress when my phone started ringing. It was this dumb bitch, Courtney, so I answered it because I'd been wondering when she'd call me crying.

"You got your head out of AD's ass now?" I asked her.

"Girl, what is you talkin bout? My head was never up his ass. Thank you very much. Maybe in between his thighs, but."

"TMI bitch! When you gon come and see my new crib?" I asked her all happy and shit.

"Didn't know that you'd moved. Some friend you are." Courtney tried to make it seem like she cared and like it bothered her that I never mentioned anything about moving to her.

"You can come over whenever you want to. I just got my stuff settled in here. You gon have to mind the place cause I haven't put anything up yet. I stay in Dunwoody. Close to Perimeter," I threw in there, so she would know that I was living the fuck goodt.

"Ooohhhh! I'm so happy for you friend. Text me your address! I'm on my way. I can't wait to see it and we can go shopping for decorations," she said.

"Aight. I'mma share my location, so you'll have the addy," I told her.

"Okay. See you soon love," Courtney told me before she disconnected the call between us.

"This bitch!" I yelled as I tossed back the covers on my air mattress to straighten up before she got here.

I was cleaning and straightening up my place before she got there and wondering why Courtney was so chill about Slade's situation. She hadn't once mentioned him to me and spoke on what they were going through, so I felt like she was hiding something from me.

"Why was she being so secretive with me?" I asked myself. I thought of ways that I could make her talk to me and tell me her business like she used to and then I heard my door-bell ring. I walked over to the door and opened it to let Courtney in.

"Hey girl!" she said cheerfully.

"Hey. Come on in. It ain't much, but it's mines. I haven't done much in here yet cause I just moved in today," I said before she started telling me what I should change or what I should do to make the apartment more homie.

She had a knack for decorative things and was always in a good mood even when she was pissed off. I never thought that I'd feel this way about her. That I'd dislike and despise her, but I did. She didn't have to fucking struggle like I did, and she had people that would go out of their way to help her. I wanted her life. I looked at her and saw that she was wearing a hickey on her neck, but I knew that it wasn't from Paiton "Slade" Perez cause the hickey was fresh and he was locked the fuck up.

"New boo?" I raised my eyebrow and smiled at her. "I see I'm not the only one keeping secrets," I checked the hoe.

Courtney laughed. "Adric been acting weird lately. I

don't know why he tryna claim me girl. I'm just having fun with him and letting things flow. I'm not forcing anything or rushing into nothing with him, but we've been talking bout moving in together lately," she said.

"What about Slade? You just gon throw away what y'all had like that?"

"You must ain't heard?" she turned her lip up and became sad for a second.

Yes! I got the bitch right where I want her, I thought to myself. "Oh, he got a baby on the way. YEAH! It's Khari's ex, too, girl. Say he came to the hood and made it known he was fuckin with her about a week ago. They been fuckin. So, you done with that nigga now?" I asked her.

"Mmmhuh. AD made me change my number and got me back in school. He just done came along and made me focus on what's important instead of all the gossip and what these other bitches doing," she shook her head and laughed at herself for admitting it.

I slammed my door as we finished touring my apartment and rolled my eyes at the back of her head as I noticed her new tracks. *"Nigga bought the bitch bundles and upgraded her,"* I said to myself. Courtney turned around to look at me and I looked at her with so much jealousy and envy in my heart for her.

"Well, since you done with him, then I might as well let you know," I told her.

"Let me know what? What you got to tell me? What's it about? Slade?" Courtney asked me like she was afraid of what I was about to say to her.

"Yep. Me and Slade been fucking during y'all entire relationship. It was one time when y'all first got together, and we recently were fucking every chance that we got, but then he moved on to Khari's ex. He called me today asking me to ride for him. Girl, I love that man and I wanted to say yes but look at how he dogged your dumb ass. Then, he went and had a baby on me. That shit was unforgivable, so I told him no," I laughed in her face. "I'M SO GLAD WE HAD THIS TALK GIRL, AND I WAS ABLE TO GET THIS OFF MY CHEST!" I walked over to Courtney to hug her, but she pushed me back from her.

"Damn, you can't stand to see me happy. You did me like that Brit! You stay calling me a dumb bitch or saying that I'm stupid but look at you. Always going after a nigga that ain't yours. Your pussy must suck. You can't get a man of your own."

"It got your man hoe. It won't be long before AD do you the same way and clown your ass. Hell, this pussy so good that it might make him leave your young ass for me," I laughed again. "GET THE FUCK OUT OF MY HOUSE!" I screamed to get a reaction out of her, but she stayed calm.

"If you were my real friend, then you'd be happy for me," Courtney had the nerve to say before she walked towards my front door.

"Bitch, I secretly hate you. I can't stand you Courtney. I WAS NEVER YOUR FRIEND!" I yelled from behind her.

"I'm going to pray for you and let God handle you," she said to me with tears in her eyes.

I could tell that I'd hurt her and that we'd never ever be friends again. Damn, I'd fucked up and crossed the line. There was no way that I'd ever get my friend back because Courtney didn't forgive women easily. She'd went through a lot of fucked up shit with Slade, so she was reserved when it came to these bitches. It wasn't like she hadn't told me how she felt about friendships and warned me about doing bullshit to cross her. I never imagined that she'd be this calm when I told her how I really felt about her this whole time.

I went inside of my room and cried cause I'd lost my friend over some envious shit that could've been avoided if I'd have stayed solid. I hated the way that niggas loved my friend.

26

Adric

I was late meeting my homeboy Idris fuckin round with Teamber's ass. All she wanted from me was money and dick, but I couldn't give her that because I'm a one-woman man. I could only fuck one woman at a time cause I ain't have time for no slip-ups or accidents. Man, I was always thinking bout Courtney during the day. It didn't matter what it was that I was doing. I was on some stalker shit over lil shawty cause I wanted to know where she was at and what she was doing. If she was mad or if she was smiling, so that's how I knew that I cared about her. That's how I knew that I fell for her the first time that I saw her from the back when she was walking inside of the convenient store. She was fine as fuck then and she was gon be fine as fuck when she walked down the aisle to marry me. Yeah, that's where my head was at. I was sure about marrying and spending the rest of my life with her.

I had to end this shit with Teamber first, so I called her to see where she was at after I finished going over my plans with Idris. Teamber told me that she was at the townhouse that I'd bought for her, so I told her that I was on my way back over there to chill with her for a minute. *Fuck!* She sounded happy as fuck, but I was about to hurt her. Probably crush her soul, but she deserved better than me. She deserved a man that could give her what she wanted. She didn't want love or to settle down and be who and what I needed, and I was getting tired of waiting on her to get right for me. It ain't like she ain't know what the fuck I wanted. She just was comfortable with a nigga thinking that she was the shit and that another hoe couldn't snatch me from her, but Courtney had done that shit just by being herself.

Courtney didn't even want me when I tried to get at her. She gave me something to do when I felt like Teamber wasn't stun me. Courtney gave me, something to pursue and she made life fun for me. She gave me a purpose... to make her want me.

I pulled up and hopped out my ride to go and break the news to Teamber. My stomach was in knots cause I knew she wasn't going to be ready for this shit. We weren't together, but she claimed me like I was her man, so this was going to be a hard pill for her to swallow.

"What's up?" I asked her when she opened the door for me. "You must was looking out for a nigga?"

"Why you say that?" Teamber asked me.

"You came to the door before I could knock or ring the doorbell," I told her.

"AD, you know I couldn't wait to see you. I peeped out the blinds and saw your car pull up, but I wasn't looking out for you. You just happened to be pulling up when I checked to see if you were outside yet. I missed you," she said.

Teamber walked up to me and wrapped her arms around my neck to stare me inside my eyes before she tried to kiss me.

"Hell nawl!" I shook my head from side to side. "You know we don't do no kissin no more. You ain't my girl and ion know who dick you been suckin. Get back girl."

"That's how you feel?" she tilted her head to the side and looked at me like I'd called her a hoe or something.

"I need to tell you something. You might wanna sit down for this. Alright?" I waited for her to answer me.

"What? What you got to tell me? Something good, I hope," Teamber walked over to the couch in her living room and sat down on one of the cushions.

I sat down beside her, placed my hand on her knees and looked her dead in her eyes.

"I'm seeing someone else now," I told her.

Teamber's ass could've been a damn actress cause she didn't need the mascara that actresses used to make themselves tear up. She put her face down, covered her face in her hands, and then her shoulders went to jerking. I sat there looking at her, trying to figure out if she was crying for real, or tryna make a nigga feel bad for letting her know that her time was up.

"Move your hands from your face!" I demanded.

She uncovered her face and I could see her makeup stained from her tears.

"Is it her? The young girl that ran up on us in the 'jects, AD! She's a child. She's too young for you!" she complained.

"I'm ready to get married!" I screamed cause her ass was acting like she didn't hear me the first time that I'd told her ass that shit.

Teamber snapped her head back at me and caught an attitude. She stood up from the couch, before me with her hands on her hips. I was worried until she started smiling and shaking her head like she was cool.

"What does she know about holding a dope boy down?" Teamber asked me.

I hated it when she did that shit. When she underestimated my ability to find a real ass bitch that could replace her. She walked around this bitch like her shit didn't stink, and I wasn't too fond of that.

"Damn T! She a rider for real." I closed my eyes and thought about how Courtney rode my dick this morning. "She knows enough. Don't let her concern you. You don't need to worry about her. We good. It's over between us though. I still got love for you, but I'm bout to propose to my lil shawty," I told her.

"Okay. You still gon let me keep the house?"

"Ion care. You can keep it, or you can move. After we get married, then you've gotta move out and get in yo own shit," I told her. "It won't look right, me paying yo bills, and I'm married to another bitch. Plus, I haven't told Courtney shit bout you and me." I ran my hands up and down my face in frustration cause I had to come clean and tell Courtney bout my other bitch.

"Aight. Go, nigga. I can't believe you'd hurt me like this. I'll always love you and be here for you Adric. This supposed to be us," she flexed her middle and index finger back and forth as if she was pointing between the both of us.

"Naw, yeen want me when you had me. All you wanted is the dick and the lil change that I threw yo way. You'n want true love. It was yours and you neglected it. Somebody else had to come and get it before you realized what the fuck you had boo." I opened her front door and left her ass with something to think about.

She wasn't about to make me feel bad for her giving up on us and not wanting what I had to offer when I was tryna be a good man to her and give her all I had. Teamber was too calm, so I had to leave before she nutted up on me, but I knew that she was plotting something. She was petty and messy like that, where she'd do some spiteful shit to ruin what I had going on. That's why I was single cause she sabotaged all my relationships and ran bitches away. These hoes thought that she was my main bitch or the woman that was holding me down when she wasn't shit but a bird that I fucked with for convenience.

I was in my car thinking about Courtney and tryna figure out how I was going to tell her about my situation with Teamber. I wouldn't be able to handle it if she told me that she didn't want to continue getting to know me and quit fucking with me, but I had questions and reservations when it came down to me and her too.

"Is she over her ex? Is she ready to marry me?" I repeatedly asked myself on my drive to her apartment.

I had to know, so I called her and got mad when I noticed that she'd been crying. I'd been watching her like a hawk, so I knew how her voice sounded and listened to cues when I was talking to her. I love her so much, but I was scared as fuck cause I'd never imagine that it was this possible to love someone as much as I loved Courtney.

"Why you cryin? Who did it?" I asked her after she sniffled and said hello.

"I-I don't want to talk about it. I got into it with my friend. That's all," she told me.

"Where you at?"

"I'm about to be at home."

"I'm pulling up," I told her.

"Okay, I just parked," she laughed, so I chilled out and pressed my foot further down on the gas pedal.

I pulled up and parked my car a short distance away from hers. I noticed that she was walking towards her building, so I hurriedly got out of my car and rushed over to her. I turned her around and grabbed her by her face, so that I could stare at her beauty. I was in love with every-thing about Courtney. She was perfect, but I could tell that she'd been crying, so I wiped the tears from her face. I kissed her and forced myself not to close my eyes as I locked lips with her. She kissed me back and wrapped her arms around my waist, so that made me feel wanted and desired. Courtney was good at showing me the love and affection that I craved from every other bitch that I chose to fuck with. She was so different, nothing like these other women, and I was ready to tell her how I felt about her.

"I missed you so much. Tell me that you ain't crying ova yo ex," I said for confirmation.

"I'm not crying over him." She screwed up her face and took a step back from me.

"You mean that shit?" I took two steps forward towards her until we were face to face again.

I placed my arms around her and pulled her closer into my chest.

"Baby, I love you. Only you. I'm done with him. Ain't no goin back. Bae? Believe me," she said to me.

My heart did flips inside of my chest and sped up at

the sound of her saying that shit to me. I had no other choice, but to do it. I knelt in front of her and took her hand inside of mines to propose to her.

"Courtney. Will you make me the happiest man in the world and marry me?" I asked her.

She rolled her eyes, sighed, and then she smirked at me. *This girl was going to turn me down or leave me standing at the altar,* I thought. Courtney was always playing games with niggas, but she wasn't going to play with me like she did them other niggas.

"YES! Yes, I will Adric. I lllloooovvveeee yyyyooouuu." She leaned her head down and kissed me before she helped me up.

I carried her inside of her apartment and fucked the shit out of her until we both fell asleep. We had to turn our phones off for this shit, and I was up, back at it, fucking her to sleep again when daybreak came in. I didn't want to wait any longer because I knew that she was the one for me, so we went to the Justice of Peace and got married once we got up. Courtney and I filed our paperwork, so that we were legally married in the state of Georgia and then we went through a roadblock on the way back to her apartment. I complied and gave the officer my license and registration at the checkpoint, but I was told that there was a warrant out for my arrest. The fuck ass police didn't tell me what I had a warrant out for, but they were more than happy to lock my ass up though. I couldn't keep my eyes off her face when they cuffed me because her face was the only face that I'd ever need to see in this lifetime. I was obsessed with the girl; she was my obsession, and I loved her voice. I'd married an angel in real life.

"I didn't mean for this to happen like this baby," I told her before I was escorted to the squad car.

27

Courtney

I was sitting there in the passenger seat lost as fuck cause AD had just been detained for nothing. My mind was racing a mile a minute because I didn't know what to do, but people were honking their horns behind me. I jumped from the sound of someone knocking on the driver's window, but it was the police. It was funny how they were clearing out the area and the roadblock was over now that they had Adric in custody.

"Were they looking for him or something?" I asked myself.

"Ma'am, you've got to drive the car," one of the offi-cers told me.

I nodded my head that I understood him and then I opened the passenger door, so I could get in the driver's seat and drive myself home. My heart was hurting, and I was disappointed because we'd just gotten married and now my other half was gone. They just up and took him from me when I least expected it, and I ain't know what to do but cry. I cried all the way home and sat in my bed, eating snacks, watching TV, and checking my phone for a phone call from a number that I didn't recognize. I waited up all night for Adric to call me, but I guessed that he wasn't given a phone call.

I started thinking the worst. *Did he use his phone call to call somebody else? Did they brutally assault him like they did these other Black men in the United States?* I pulled my pillow close to my chest and cried myself to sleep because I was missing him. I didn't have a piece of his clothing with his scent to keep with me, so I was going crazy.

My phone ringing woke me up the next morning, so I rolled over and yawned before I looked at my phone screen. "I wonder who this is calling me?" I asked myself aloud.

My ring on my finger reminded me of what happened yesterday. I got married, but my husband was locked up, and I was waiting for his phone call, so I answered the phone. I closed my eyes and said a quick prayer that it was Adric on the other end of the line.

"Uuummm… Hello?" My voice was raspy from being sleep, and it cracked as I got my words out.

"Aye bae! My bad. I mean, wife. Go to the door. It's moving day!" He was excited and shit, so I moaned and slid out the bed to follow his commands and go to the door.

"Huh? Where am I moving to? What? Adric!" I squealed.

"I got us a house before we tied the knot cause I knew that you and I were going to need somewhere to build our bond and start a family. Somewhere new. A place fresh without the memories in your apartment," he told me.

"What?" I looked at the movers suspiciously when they walked past me to start moving things out of my apartment. "Huh? What are these people doing? Where are they taking my stuff? Bbbaabbbyy!" I whined.

"Yeah, it's real. Did you get the flowers that I sent you?" he asked me.

I walked to the door and there was a big vase of my favorite flowers... daisies.

"Mrs. Hernandez?" A man asked.

I had to look down at my ring again before I realized that we'd really did this shit. I'd married the man of my dreams, but I got saddened at the thought of him not being here with me. I missed him, and I wanted to see him. I wanted to run to him and give him a hug. I needed to kiss him and tell him how much I loved him cause he was always doing simple shit to put a smile on my face. Adric was good at making me let down my guard and laugh like there was no one else around me.

"Yes," I answered the man that was dropping off the flowers.

"I have some edible arrangements for you as well Mrs. Hernandez. Sign right here," he directed me.

I signed the clipboard stating that I'd received the edible arrangement and flowers, and then I gave my attention back to my husband.

"Baby, let me come see you. Can we video chat or something?" I asked him. I plopped down on my sofa and tore into the fruit and chocolates.

He knew me so damn well. Adric knew that I hardly ate because I was self-conscious about my weight and I disliked breakfast food. It was the small things that he didn't think that I paid attention to that made my heart jump out my chest for him. I fell in love with him over and over each day. I sometimes wished that I'd met him sooner in life.

"No, you'll see me in due time, when I come home. Until then, move yo ass into our new crib. Bye, I love you," he told me.

"I love you too." I said in a low tone with no cheer evident in my voice.

"Don't sound like that. I hate when you be acting all ungrateful. You love me Mrs. Hernandez?"

"I love you husband," I told him.

"That's better. You fuckin wit a street nigga. Don't make me feel like you'n appreciate me," he said.

"Yes daddy." I munched on some fruit and rolled my eyes up at the ceiling. *And you dealing with a street bitch,*" I said to myself.

"Woo!" Adric said before the phone call ended.

The movers instructed me to follow them to my new house that Mr. Hernandez had bought for me as a gift. I tossed on some decent clothes to go out in and then I got inside of his car to see what this new house looked like. It was beautiful and exactly what I wanted. Something for us to start in because I didn't want much. I just wanted a house to call a home. A place to call my own. Adric had a four-bedroom, three-bathroom house built from the ground up for me. He'd been paying attention to the little things that I'd told him while we were laying up and pillow talking. He was so fuckin' charming and attentive.

"Damn, why he gotta be locked up?" I cried inside my head. My husband was tryna get his dick sucked good for surprising me like that. I'd been listening to him, too, so I knew what he wanted me to do.

I thanked the movers and got the two sets of house keys from them before I locked up the house. I drove back to my apartment and felt lonely as fuck, so I started googling things that I could do to occupy my damn time. I'd already re-enrolled in school, so I completed some homework assignments. I realized that all of my belongings were now inside of the house that Adric had gotten for us, so I left my apartment to go to stay the night in my new home. Settling into the house was easier than I could have ever imagined, yet I was lonely. It was my first night alone in the house, and all I wanted was my fuckin husband beside me.

Adric had no bond and had to go before the judge before he could get any information on what he was being held for and the amount that he'd need to put up to get out. I got on my shit and found a side hustle by doing hair at my old apartment and busied myself with decorating our house to make it a home. I found myself missing Britin at times, but I didn't need a foe for a friend, so I chose to stay in my lane and ride my own wave. I made a few friends through my clients, but I knew not to play with Adric, so I stayed home doing wife shit.

Today, he'd called me and woke me up real early, so I got up and made myself some breakfast.

"Damn, I've gotta give this nigga a baby," I giggled when I finished cooking.

I had more than enough food left over, so I fixed two

breakfast plates just in case I had a client come through hungry this morning. I'd let them warm their plate up and eat before I started on their head. My doorbell rang, and I frowned up because no one knew where I lived, and I didn't do hair at the house.

I skipped to the door to answer it. *I've seen her before*, I thought to myself.

"Are you Mrs. Hernandez?" the woman asked me.

"Yes, I am. How can I help you?"

"You may be Adric's wife, but I'm his girlfriend, Teamber. You might remember me from the last time you tried to pull up on him and check him about who the fuck I was to him," she said to me before she continued. "But, I'm his longtime girlfriend," the woman laughed. "I know all about you. He shows mmmaaaddddd love to yo ugl ass, but that's okay. That's alright. I wanted to come and formally introduce myself to you since my town house that he paid for is being renovated. Our man is locked up, and I haven't video chatted with him today. I came by here to ask you to go inside of his safe, the one in y'all bedroom upstairs. You know where it is right? Behind the TV that's mounted up against the wall. Yeah, go in there and give me something to hold me over until I can move back into my townhouse or I could just come and stay wit you," Teamber said to me

"Wait, what? Come again?" I shook my head and furrowed my eyebrows cause I just knew that I had to be tripping. She wasn't trying me wit the fuck shit.

"Bitch, stop acting like you deaf. That nigga ain't goin nowhere. He wifed you up cause he was desperate. I know he cheats and that he can't be faithful, but who he comes home to? Me or you?" she asked me with a smirk on her face. "At least I get to see him. You ole dumb sideline hoe," the woman said to me.

"BITCH!" I yelled before I blacked out on her ass. *"How did she know where his safe was in our new crib?"* I asked myself as I beat her ass.

The neighbors came outside and pulled us away from each other.

"I suggest you take this up with Adric. I've already gotten my phone call from him today. I told him that I'd come and confront you if he didn't stop playing games with me. Have you heard from him? Oh, is that a wedding ring on your finger?" the woman that I remembered from the projects kept eyeing me and snapping on me.

"Ring, ring, ring!" My cell phone's ringtone was ringing in my back pocket.

I grimaced and answered the phone as I breathed heavily.

"ADRIC! BABY! YOU BETTER TELL ME SOME-THING!" I screamed through the phone at him.

"What? What is it?" he asked from the other end of the phone.

"I thought you said that you were gonna give them a reason to hate me!" I looked down at my ring contemplating if being the wife of a street nigga was even worth it.

"Would it always be this way?" I asked myself.

"ADRIC! WHAT'S UP NIGGA?" Teamber yelled as the police pulled up inside of my driveway.

"Whose residence is this?" The officers asked us.

"Baby! What the fuck is going on?" Adric asked me.

"You better pray I don't divorce your ass," I told him.

I ended the phone call and tried to kill this woman, Teamber that came to our house being disrespectful to me and my husband.

To be continued.

Connect with me on Facebook @ Tonya Williams and Instagram @tonyathewriter

Subscribe

Text Shan to 22828 to stay up to date with new releases, sneak peeks, contest, and more....

Submissions

To submit your manuscript to Shan Presents, please send
the first three chapters and synopsis to
submissions@shanpresents.com

CPSIA information can be obtained
at www.ICGtesting.com
Printed in the USA
LVHW031700171219
640803LV00002B/363/P